AF410314

Sparks, S'mores, And Scandals

Books by

Michelle L. Clifton

Taryn O'Kelly Mysteries

Party Planning for Murder (Book 1)
Frost and Foul Play (Novella 1.5)
Cruises, Cocktails, and Corpses (Book 2)
Sparks, S'mores, and Scandals (Book 3)

Sparks, S'mores, And Scandals

Michelle L. Clifton

SaltyInspirations.com

Copyright © 2026 by Salty Inspirations

All rights reserved. No portion of this book may be reproduced in any form without written permission from the publisher or author, except as permitted by U.S. copyright law.

Published in the United States by Salty Inspirations

All Salty Inspirations titles are available for purchase through SaltyInspirations.com

Library of Congress Control Number: 2026906200

ISBN: 979-8-9908817-8-5 (Paperback)

ISBN: 979-8-9908817-7-8 (E-pub)

Printed in the United States, Britain, Canada, & Australia.

Cover Design by Michelle Clifton

Salty Inspirations

Cape Coral, FL 33904

www.saltyinspirations.com

For my son,
a firefighter who runs toward danger when others must run away.
Your courage, strength, and quiet determination inspire me more than words can say.
And to the VFW,
thank you for keeping the spirit and memories of our heroes alive for generations to come.

Chapter 1

S ummer in the Colorado Rockies is the perfect time of year. Technically, it's not summer yet; we are coming out of mud season. Mud season, you ask? Well, Colorado has seven seasons: summer, fall, Indian summer, winter, frigid winter, trying to be spring, first mud, second winter, second mud, and summer! It may have 360 days of sunshine, but a lot of good that does when you can only go outside for 250 days of the year.

That's what tropical vacations are for, right? I thought that too until my romantic cruise getaway with Alex took a wrong turn. What was supposed to be a warm, relaxing paradise was off the table. We had a run-in with the cartel, and things got deadly.

I'm Taryn O'Kelly, and I am an event coordinator. Don't get me wrong, I love Colorado. Silver Springs air is so fresh and crisp, and smells of pine trees. When you smell pine trees, you probably think of Christmas. But when I smell them, I think of hiking trails, camping, and wilderness adventures.

Currently, we are in the second mud season, and the raindrops pelting my metal roof had me annoyed. My KOA campground reopening picnic and barbecue was to start in four days. The weather forecast for the weekend predicted nothing but rain. I watched trails of water run down the windowpanes. Peering out past the rain into the gloomy clouds with my hands on my hips, I sighed. I didn't notice Alex coming into my office. His warm hand touched me, settling on my shoulder, surprising me.

"I didn't mean to startle you. What's bothering you?" His face was filled with concern.

"Oh, my event is about to be rained out, and that woodpecker is pissing me off." I pointed to the crazy woodpecker pecking the crap out of my poor ash tree out front.

"You're not the only one who wants that woodpecker gone." Alex pointed to my cat Giselle, the fluffy ball of orange fur who was bobbing her head and flattening her face against the window, hoping a magical portal would open so she could attack through the glass.

"She's irritated with him, too!" I smiled, patting her on the head. She tried to avoid the pat, as if breaking her eye contact with the annoying bird would lessen her supernatural chances of catching him beyond her glass barrier.

Alex wrapped his arms around me. "You always worry about things you have no control over. If it's rained out, it's not your fault."

"I know, but I love the KOA campground. Plus, this is the town's official *summer is here party*. I want summer to be here," I whined, leaning back into his embrace.

"There's a backup date; the party will still happen. You need to take a break. Glaring at the clouds and the bird will change nothing for you." He smiled.

"True, but I like glaring at them. It makes me feel like I have a little control," I grumbled.

I stayed wrapped in his arms for a bit longer, trying to relax into him and think only about the moment, but the annoying thoughts of rescheduling and that woodpecker refused to leave my brain.

I blew out a sigh, wiggled my way out of his embrace, but not without kissing him first. "I have a few more things to do for work, then I will take that break you suggested." I smiled. "Plus, I need to head over to the campground and check in with Ryan."

"Do you want me to tag along?"

"I would love for you to tag along!"

I watched Alex exit the room. He had a very nice butt, and that was distracting enough to forget about the stupid woodpecker. At least until he disappeared from sight. I glared one last time at the woodpecker and the clouds, hoping they both would go away. No such luck.

Resuming my seat at my desk, I wrapped up a few things for other events I had coming up that I hoped mud season wouldn't ruin.

After completing the tasks I needed to, I slipped on my hiking boots. Just a few weeks earlier, I was in flip-flops. It's hard to go back to boots when you've been in flip-flops. I sighed, reached for my coat, and hollered to Alex, letting him know I was ready to go.

We raced down the steps to my truck, trying our best to dodge the raindrops. Our attempts were futile. There were just too many of them.

Alex was driving, so I settled into the passenger seat, finger-combing my wet, wavy, auburn hair, trying to fluff it up so I didn't look like a drowned rat.

While Alex backed the truck out of the driveway, I noticed the woodpecker taking a break, nestling himself further into the crook of a tree branch. I guess Giselle will get a break from stalking him too.

"Did you read in the paper that the Collins sold their farm to that investment firm? Apparently, they are going to mainstream the farm, letting the Collins keep a commission." Alex asked as we turned north onto Main street heading towards the edge of town.

"No, but the Smuckers sold theirs to the same company a few months ago. I don't know what's going on, but I don't like these huge companies buying up our tiny patch of paradise." I furrowed my brows in thought.

"I don't trust them either. Every time these big companies come to small towns, it ends up hurting the people more than it helps," Alex replied.

Our conversation was interrupted by the sound of sirens. I looked in the rearview mirror as Alex pulled off to the side to let the fire trucks pass. They were heading in the same direction we were. Saying a silent prayer for whoever was involved, I asked their guardian angels, all the saints, and God to keep them safe.

"Look at this jerk!" Alex gestured to a car ahead of us that wasn't moving out of the way. The firetruck's horn blared as it flew past us, approaching the car. The driver finally started to move out of the way, but not before the firetruck started braking so as not to hit him.

"I hate it when people do that! They would be very unhappy if it were their life on the line and someone blocked the road to their rescue." I glared at the car's owner.

Alex pulled our truck back onto the road, careful to watch for more rescue vehicles trying to pass. As we followed the firetruck down, we noticed they were taking the same country road we were. My stomach started to turn. Was the KOA campground the scene of the incident?

Trailing behind, I peered out the window, hoping to see something. Then, as the camp came into sight, I could see black, billowing smoke.

"I really hope everyone's okay." A small panic was rising in me.

"The smoke looks further from the camp, maybe the property behind it?" Alex suggested, winding us down the country road.

He was right! It wasn't the camp! The firetrucks blasted past the entrance, continuing down the road towards the bridge. The Winterburn River runs through Silver Springs. At the northern end of town, there is a bridge connecting the west and east river bank with sparse country homes and farms filling the landscape on both sides.

I wanted so badly to follow the Firetrucks, but I knew we shouldn't. Plus, my brother is a firefighter. I can find out what happened from him. Alex parked the truck in front of the campground office. It was a little rustic building with a covered porch. An iron bench stretched across half of it. The firewood shed next to the building was bigger and already fully stocked for the campers. Large 100-year-old spruce trees shaded the little office; their pine needles had been raked and removed, revealing the path down to the river. Spring cleaning was almost done.

Hauling ourselves out of the truck, we rushed to the porch. Stomping my feet and wiping them on the front mat, I opened the door and entered the building. Alex followed behind me. The office served as a little shop, too. The left side had snacks and toiletries, and the right side had souvenirs and trinkets from local artisans.

There was a tiny desk stuffed into the back corner. Rosie was behind the checkout counter refilling the pamphlet wheel with campground maps, trail guides, and excursion packages from around Silver Springs.

"Hi Taryn," she greeted me, peering behind me towards Alex. She blushed. Alex is tall, dark, and handsome in every sense of the word. He has olive skin, honey-colored eyes, brown, almost black hair, and every bit of him is well-toned muscle. He's a private detective, a pilot, and a former Air Force pilot. He also happens to be my boyfriend.

"Rosie, this is Alex." I motioned behind me.

Alex came to my side, placing his hand on the small of my back and shaking Rosie's with the other.

"Nice to meet you, Rosie." He smiled.

Rosie giggled before pulling herself together and saying hi. She was younger than me, twenty, I think. She had black curly hair, pulled into a messy bun, and stray, perfect ringlet curls fell out everywhere. She could play Snow White if she straightened her hair.

"I heard sirens a few minutes ago. Was there an accident?" Rosie asked, returning her attention to the pamphlet stand.

"We could see smoke, and the firetrucks were headed towards the bridge, but we don't know much else," I replied.

Alex had wandered over to the souvenir section and was handling a railroad spike.

Rosie watched him. I rolled my eyes. Good grief.

"I have come to check in with Ryan," I said, trying to catch the girl's attention.

"He's out on the tractor cleaning out the last of the brush and smoothing out the campsites. We are booked solid for the weekend." Rosie mumbled, clearly still very distracted by Alex.

"That's wonderful news!" I clapped my hands together.

"It is. Do you want me to radio him?" Rosie motioned towards the walkie-talkie sitting on the back counter.

"No, I'll go find him. I need to walk the property one more time anyway. But thank you."

Rosie frowned, her eyes returning to Alex. "You'll get wet."

"We won't melt," I replied, moving towards Alex.

Alex replaced the railroad spike, grabbing my hand. "Ready, then?"

"Yep, bye, Rosie." I waved.

"Bye," she sighed. "Hey, stop back by if you get a chance!" She bounced on her heels.

We exited the shop. Standing under the porch, I pulled my hood up, tucking as much hair beneath it as possible.

"That girl is crazy! She was so distracted by you that she had trouble filling the pamphlet stand," I scoffed.

"Jealous?" He smiled, tucking a small strand of my hair I missed into the hood, brushing his warm hand across my cheek.

"Only a little." I wrinkled my nose.

The rain was slowing down. I couldn't see the smoke plume as we could from the road. The trees here are too thick. Grabbing Alex's hand, I stepped off the porch, pulling him behind me. We took the path towards the river and the campground pavilion. I could hear the tractor groaning in the distance.

"This is nice," Alex said, pulling me to a stop.

"What is?" I looked around, confused.

"This, us strolling through the forest, no investigations, no drama, just quiet." He leaned in, kissing me.

"It is," I whispered as his lips pulled away from mine.

We stood still, peering into each other's eyes for a moment longer before continuing down the path.

Ryan, the owner of the KOA camp, was clearing the oak brush from around the pavilion. Pulling the tractor to a stop, he left it idling, waving to us before dismounting.

"Hi, Ryan." I greeted him with a hug. "This is Alex. Alex, Ryan." I motion between them. They greeted each other with a handshake.

We took shelter under the little roof.

"Things are looking nice around here," I said, "If this rain stops, it's going to be an excellent weekend."

"It sure will, as long as the fires stop happening." He said, casting a nervous glance over his shoulder.

I followed Ryan's gaze in the direction of the smoke. It was hard to tell what was smoke and what were clouds, but you could smell it in the air.

"This is the second fire out here this week." He furrowed his brow. "I didn't believe them when they said insurance rates had risen because of the fire danger. Just last week, I was talking to Lonnie Stevenson, who owns the farm bordering the edge of my property. He said his insurance company dropped him. Told him it was too expensive to insure him in such a high-risk area. Now he can't find affordable insurance. He's actually looking into letting that Little Helper Farm Company take over for him." Ryan furrowed his brow deeper in thought.

"No, he can't do that. Pretty soon, a huge corporation will own the whole valley. There's got to be something we can do. Plus, I didn't think we had lightning, and everything is still plenty wet from winter. The snowpack was good this year, too. The river shouldn't peak for weeks." My eyes drifted towards the sparkling river flowing behind me. "The fire danger should be low this year."

"I thought the same thing. We haven't had any lightning, but just a few days ago the Martins' property had a fire. Thankfully, they were home when it happened and started attending to it right away. It was so close to their house that it could have gone very badly." Ryan's face was filled with concern.

"The paper mentioned that this morning," Alex chimed in. "I was reading an article they put out saying this season has the makings to be one of the worst. There were already comments saying to close the forest, shut down the train, and ban wood burning." Alex rolled his eyes.

"That's wonderful," Ryan grumbled. "My business thrives on all those things."

"How can they predict that? They have no idea what this season will bring. It's scare tactics. We will do what we need to do, and the campground will do wonderfully this year!" I smiled. "The grand reopening will remind people of why we live here."

"I sure hope so. With the insurance rates rising and the call for closing the forest, I won't survive this year. I'd better get back to cleaning out the oak brush. If we do end up with a bad fire season, this stuff will be kindling."

"See, you are a responsible property owner; they should give you a discount for that."

"Let's hope they do. Between the insurance and pressure from Camp World trying to buy this place, my stress load is full."

"They are still bothering you?" I asked.

"Not recently, but every few weeks they touch base with me to see if I have changed my mind." He shrugged.

"Hmm, well, let me know if you need anything. Everything is all set on my end, as long as this rain stops."

"Will do. Alex, it was nice meeting you." Ryan smiled and waved goodbye.

"Nice meeting you as well."

We walked down the little path back to the truck.

"Let's drive by the fire on the way home," I suggested.

Alex pulled the truck back onto the main road, taking a right out of the driveway. From there, we could see the smoke. We followed the county road over the trestle bridge. Up ahead, the road was blocked by police and emergency vehicles, and smoke filled the air, making it hard to see. Not wanting to be in the way, Alex pulled a U-turn and took us home.

Chapter 2

"What do you think is going on with these fires?" I asked.

"I am not sure. You can get hidden lightning and have fires start without seeing or hearing the strike. Especially in storms as we have had. They're called cold-core thunderstorms. The thick clouds and constant rain can hide the lightning," Alex explained while backing the truck into my driveway.

"Well, I didn't know that. Maybe we really are going to have a bad fire season?" I reached for the handle. "But we have seen enough weird stuff that I still want to talk to Scotty and see what he knows."

"It doesn't hurt. Are you ready to run?" Alex smiled, pulling his hood up.

"Let's." I pulled the handle, jumped out of the truck, and took off running. Taking the steps two at a time, I beat Alex to the door. As I was fumbling with my keys, my front door swung open. I screamed, startled to see my ex, Robert, standing inside my house, welcoming me into my own home.

"I didn't mean to scare you. I saw you pull up and didn't want you trapped in the rain." He stepped back to let us in.

"How are you in my house?" I stepped into the foyer and carefully hung my wet coat on the coat rack, making sure that if it dripped, it dripped on the tile and nothing else.

Alex hung his coat the same way. "Hi Robert, why are you here?" He sounded less than thrilled.

"Don't worry, guys, he didn't steal a key again." Kandice came out of the kitchen.

"Yet," Robert said under his breath.

I narrowed my eyes at him. "Don't even think about it," I said, pointing at him.

"He came in with me. He brought you coffee, but I made him get Alex and me a coffee before I let him enter," she said, holding up a couple of mochas.

"She's mean. I had a coffee for you, just the way you like it, too. I was coming to see how your day was and SHE," he pointed towards Kandice, "wouldn't let me in until I came back with coffee for them too."

"It's nice to share, Robert," Kandice said, taking a seat at my table and motioning for us to join.

"Did you hear that? Nice to share." He winked at me, turning his smirk to Alex, before taking his seat.

Alex silently stared at Robert, no expression on his face. I am sure he was second-guessing his choice to hang with us once again.

"Okay, you two, enough. Robert, thank you for the coffee. Kandice, thanks for babysitting Robert."

"Hey," Robert started to protest, but I held my hand up, taking a seat next to Kandice.

Alex chose to lean against the bar.

"This is nice," I said.

My condo has an open concept living room, dining room, and kitchen. Directly across from the foyer, through the dining area, I have a balcony that overlooks the Winterburn River. There is a pellet stove in the far corner of the living room, and my kitchen is U-shaped with a bar that keeps it open to the whole room.

Kandice had the paper open to the obituaries. I noticed a few names that were circled in red.

"Why are you reading and circling the obituaries?" I asked.

"Because she wants to find another murder!" Robert blurted out.

"No, no, no, I don't want you two involved in any more investigations." Alex moved and stood behind us. "There have been too many already. I should not have to count on my hand the number of times I could have lost you." He said firmly, towering from above.

"I agree with Alex. No more, ladies." Robert puffed himself up, trying to look as big and bad as Alex.

"As if you two have any say." Kandice jabbed.

I rolled my eyes. "Enough, all of you. Let's enjoy our coffee and look at what Kandice wanted us to look at." I directed my attention to Kandice. "We do not need to start looking for trouble. We already have enough without asking for it."

"My point exactly." Robert seconded me.

"Robert, remember how we talked about not being annoying? You're failing right now. Thank you for the coffee, it was kind," I said.

He grabbed a chair and scooted it closer to me. Leaning across me, brushing my boob with his arm, he grabbed a section of the paper, settling in to read it. I rolled my eyes. Alex's facial expression said he had given up. He chose to lean against the counter once again and watch us. Kandice proceeded to explain to me why she had circled each one and why we should investigate their deaths.

"Carrie Cartwright died at age 48 from a heart attack. She was recently divorced. Maybe the ex killed her? Or," she pointed to the next circled name, "this one, Jack Hickory, died at age 82, but he had money and a lot of family. Maybe someone killed him for his money?" Kandice looked eager for someone to agree.

The three of us stared at her.

"Oh, come on, guys," she complained.

I reached my hand out, placing it on top of hers. "You make very good points, but there is no reason to believe that any of these people were murdered. Nothing has been said around town or in the paper that's suspicious."

Robert leaned back into his chair, opened the paper fully, gave it a flick, and smacked me in the face with the edge.

"Hey," I smacked at the paper inching into my personal space. "Move over."

"You tell me to go get more coffee. I'm not allowed to agree with him," he said, pointing to Kandice, then Alex. "I have to stop being annoying, although I don't know how you came to that conclusion. And now, I can't read the paper!"

"If we are so mean," Kandice drew the word out, "then why do you insist on hanging out with us? And touching Taryn's boob. And smacking her with the paper is not reading, FYI."

"Because someone needs to watch over you. Look, you're trying to find reasons to go after murderers! That is why I tolerate your abuse," Robert huffed.

A buzzing sound interrupted our argument. Everyone went silent to hear where the sound was coming from. On the counter was Alex's phone. It danced around the kitchen island, buzzing.

"This is Alexander," he said, taking the phone into my office. My condo has two bedrooms. The one off of the kitchen/dining room I had turned into my office.

"What do you really think about these deaths?" Kandice continued.

"I think the boys are right," I replied

"Ha," Robert interjected.

"That's your problem right there," I said, glaring at Robert, "Stop."

"Fine," he went back to reading the paper.

"What if the boys are wrong?" Kandice asked.

"They're not; we don't need to go looking for trouble," I said pointedly, taking another sip of my coffee.

Giselle poked her head out of my office, walked a couple of steps with her front feet, and stretched as far as her long body would go. She yawned, returning to a seated position in the middle of the doorway. Meowing, she waltzed over to me and pawed at my chair.

"Ah, does my kitty need a hug?" I picked her up and hugged her. She nestled into my lap until Robert decided to aggressively scruff her fur up. She glared at him, shook off his cooties, left my lap, and headed to the bedroom.

"Fine, if you don't think there is anything here, then we won't investigate." Kandice pouted.

We sat in silence for a minute, enjoying our coffee. I looked out the window, and the rain had not stopped.

"Hey, there's an article in the paper about a missing insurance adjuster. He recently denied claims and canceled policies on several homes in the valley. He had spoken at the last couple of city council meetings, but no one has seen him." Robert pointed at the paper.

"Is that the guy who does the local commercials for getting your house insurance proof in all seasons?" I asked.

"I remember that guy. He was annoying," Kandice chimed in.

"Yep, that's the one. Reed Jackson," Robert added. "I go to the city council meetings most of the time, and he was always pushing for zoning changes, adding insurance requirements, and even trying to get code changes in place. He was a real pile of crap."

"What's the paper say happened?" I asked, reaching for the paper.

"Nothing really, just that his housekeeper reported that he hasn't been home in a few days, and there's no way to contact him. She filed a missing persons report." Robert answered, showing me the article.

"It looks like we do have something to investigate!" Kandice bounced in her seat.

"Good riddance, I say. That guy was costing the people of Silver Springs a lot more money. A couple of months ago, a neighbor of mine put in a claim for ice damaging her roof, and this dirtbag denied her claim, saying her roof was old, anyway. She tried to fight them but eventually gave up," Robert huffed.

"I have heard people saying he was a shyster. He was new here, too, wasn't he?" I skimmed the article as Robert held it.

"Yeah, some city transplant here temporarily to update our country ways." Robert sneered, folding the paper and placing it on the table.

"The Martins just hired me to find out who tried to torch their house," Alex announced, returning to the table and taking a seat.

"What? They think it was arson, not lightning?" I asked.

"What's going on?" Kandice asked, looking confused.

"Yeah, fill us in," Robert replied, sitting up straight and folding the paper.

"The Martins own a piece of property in the valley. There was a fire a few days ago, and the paper announced that the fire season is going to be bad this year. No one has seen lightning, and there have been two fires now. That, coupled with the insurance rates rising and dropping owners, is making it easier for large corporations to buy up the land out there. The Martins are one of only a few left," I explained.

"Coincidence, I think not." Robert tapped the paper.

"So, what do you know?" I asked Alex.

"Not much yet. The fire investigator is still writing the report. Brian Martin suspects it will come back as arson, not lightning. He wants me to see if I can find any proof, just in case this comes back in a way that doesn't sit right."

"And you guys thought there was nothing to investigate. Now we have two cases." Kandice took a long, satisfying sip of her coffee.

"Two cases?" Alex asked.

"She wants us to look into the missing insurance agent and now help you." I smirked, knowing full well he was probably trying not to self-combust. I love him, but it's a little funny how we drive him crazy.

"Kandice, honey," Alex said, reaching for her hand. "No, the arson case is my job. You guys can't do anything with it. If I find something you can do to help, I will let you know."

"But we are good at this," she protested.

"Taryn, help me out here," Alex pleaded with me.

"Kandice, Alex is right. This time it's different. He was hired to do this; we can't mess with it. It would be like me planning a party, and I had cupcakes ordered, but you brought your own, removing mine."

"Cupcakes, really?" Kandice stared at me.

"Okay, fine. Use something else."

"Well, we will find the missing adjuster then," she sneered.

"Ha!" Robert scoffed. "I say leave him missing."

"Fine, you guys are party poopers. I came over excited about doing something fun with you." She pouted.

"Let's all plan something fun to go do. We could go to the hot springs! That would be fun!" I suggested, hoping to improve my adrenaline junkie friend's mood. Kandice is a thrill-seeker. When things get too routine, she gets antsy.

That's why she has a newfound love for murder investigations.

Kandice stared at me, taking another long sip of coffee.

"I like the hot springs idea," Robert announced.

"It's raining," Kandice pointed out.

"Well, not today, but maybe next week," I said.

We finished our coffee, and I sent Kandice and Robert home. Alex and I had work to get done.

I called my mom to see if Alex and I could squeeze in for dinner. I knew she would be delighted to see us, and she would tell me I never have to ask, but it's nice for her to have a heads-up, plus I can bring stuff if she needs it. I also wanted to know if Scotty would be there tonight, and he's supposed to be.

I changed into jeans, boots, and a nice, thick sweater. The rain had finally stopped, but it wasn't very warm out. Alex had been on several phone calls and needed to make a trip out to the Martins' home. I, of course, wanted to tag along.

"You ready?" Alex hollered down the hall to me.

"Almost," I said, brushing my hair, trying to get it to fluff up. The rain had flattened it to my head.

I came out of the room to find Alex had my coat and purse ready for me. He held out the coat, opening it so I could slide right in, and handed me my purse.

"You look beautiful, by the way." His warm smile melted me. As his soft lips brushed mine, I held on to him for just a minute.

We didn't have to run down the steps this time, but we opted to take my truck again. It was already out of the garage and would need to be tucked in tonight. It still freezes occasionally overnight.

Sliding into the passenger seat, I buckled up and let Alex drive again.

"I feel a little bad. Kandice wanted to investigate something, and I get to ride with you to your investigation," I admitted.

"You can't feel bad. I love Kandice, but if she wants to be an investigator, she needs to change professions. And you're not investigating anything. I was hired by these people to find information for them. Much of my work doesn't involve chasing down murderers, it's tracking down paperwork," Alex replied, pulling the truck out of the driveway.

"You make it sound so glamorous." I smirked. "But I still wish there was something I could do for Kandice."

We hit the highway and followed it out of town before turning onto County Road 253 for the second time today, but before passing the KOA, we turned off the main road and wound far back into the country. It was beautiful back here. The road cut through the thick, tall pine trees. Oak brush and aspen clusters were sprinkled amongst the pines. I could see a clearing up ahead. The road curved to the right, but the driveway we needed continued straight. Gravel crunched under the truck's tires as we transitioned from pavement to a country road. The Martins' driveway was long, and their house was nestled deep in the property, close to the river, making this place very secluded.

"You would have to hike in here to commit arson and not be seen," I said as the meadow grew larger.

"You're right, driving a car down here would be risky since it's the only way in and out of the property. Seeing where the fire started may point us in the right direction. There are several neighbors. I printed the plot maps. They are in the folder if you want to look at them. Once I know exactly where the fire started, I can plot paths an arsonist could have taken."

I reached for the Manila folder Alex had placed in the center console. Opening it, I pulled out a packet of papers. I was shocked to see how much information Alex was able to attain in the few hours we had before coming back out here. Information on all the close neighbors, plot maps, warranty deeds, and the date of sale.

"Wow, you've found a lot already!" I exclaimed, flipping through the file.

"That's just the preliminary legwork. Most of that won't end up being needed, but it keeps me from overlooking something," he said, smiling.

"Is it wrong that this organized Clark Kent version of you is turning me on?" I winked.

"I thought I was Batman?" He chuckled.

"Oh, you are. Batman vs Superman, for me, it's Batman all the way! I just don't know if Bruce Wayne has this hot, nerdy organizational ability." I smiled.

"As long as I am your superhero, I don't care who it is."

"Are you trying to make me forget how to breathe?

"Ha ha, I didn't realize this part of my job would be so enchanting for you."

"I didn't either. When I imagined you working, I thought more along the lines of stakeouts and sneaking around."

"Like what you and Kandice do?"

"Well, you did too, when we were on the cruise."

"Touché." He laughed. "I do stakeouts and sneaking around as well, it's just not every case. A lot of them are paper trails I dig up."

Alex pulled up to the log cabin home and parked off to the side of the garage. There was smoke coming from the chimney. Daffodils and tulips clung together in the freshly mulched garden beds. Clusters of Aspen trees stood off to the left of the cabin, and their leaf buds were just starting to open.

I climbed out of the truck, careful to stay on the gravel. The ground was soaked, and I didn't want to end up in the mud. The scent of pine, spring water, and smoke filled the air. I took a deep breath, enjoying the Colorado smell. This is why I live here, I thought to myself. Alex waited for me to come around the truck before we proceeded to walk to the front door.

"You must be Alex?" Brian Martin greeted us, opening the door.

"I am Alexander Cruz, and this is Taryn O'Kelly," he said, shaking Brian Martin's hand.

"Hello," I said, receiving the handshake.

"Please come in. My wife and son are out at the moment, but we wanted you to get started right away. The scene of the crime is only getting harder to collect evidence from as this rain continues."

Brian escorted us through the foyer and into the living room. I could see a loft above us. The vaulted ceilings and grand fireplace made the room feel larger than it was. Taking a seat closest to the fireplace, I quietly watched Alex work. He had a notepad with his notes from the earlier conversation. He dated and time-stamped everything. Pulling out his manila envelope, he took out the plot map and asked Brian to point to where the fire had started. Alex made another note.

Brian explained that the fire started on a Thursday last week. The weather conditions were similar to today's. I had a feeling Alex had already referenced the weather conditions for that day, and the info was tucked away nicely into his little magical info packet. But Alex smiled and took notes as Brian explained the events leading up to finding the fire.

"My wife and I were having our morning coffee, sitting there, at the dining room table. She had made a batch of pecan rolls," he smiled, "we were watching to see if the herd of deer that had been frequenting our back yard would show up. I had just taken a delicious, gooey bite when I could see flames. My wife started hollering for our son, who was still in bed, to come quickly. 'There's a fire!' she shouted. I was still trying to swallow the bite of sticky bun." He paused a moment, then continued. "I was in my pajamas and slippers. I told my wife to call 911 and to send Brandon out to help me. I slipped into my boots and threw on a coat. I was going to get the hose. Turning it on, I ran towards the fire. I had Brandon spraying the roof and around the house in case sparks landed. By the time the fire department got here, I had kept the fire from spreading past the main tree, but it took a bit for them to get it out."

"It certainly is a good thing you were here, that could have gotten out of control fast," Alex replied.

"Too close for comfort, that's for sure."

"Why do you feel this was arson?" Alex asked.

"I never heard or saw any lightning, and I had just argued with the insurance adjuster about how I had taken the necessary steps to keep my home as fireproof as possible while living in the middle of the forest. If you look around, I have no policy violations and have followed their 'defensible space guidelines'. My wood shed is fifteen feet from the house. It's not convenient when the snow is three feet high, but it's where they want it." Brian scowled.

"Do you remember the adjuster's name and what the carrier's name is?" Alex asked.

"The adjuster was Reed something, I remember, because I have a brother named Reed, and the carrier is Neighborhood Integrity." Brian scooted to the edge of his seat, trying to peek at what Alex was writing.

"Mr. Martin," I addressed him, "Why was the adjuster out and what day was that?" I asked, hoping Alex wouldn't mind.

I think he was shocked that I spoke, since it took him a moment to answer me. "Oh, my policy was under threat of being dropped, and they had to come out and assess the risk of insuring my home. They sent me a non-renewal letter saying, 'pending their inspection', the policy would not renew. Reed said he was to write a report on 'his findings' but wouldn't tell me what 'his findings' were. That was last Wednesday."

"Have you seen his report?" Alex asked.

"No, I haven't heard anything from him, and it's been over a week. Our policy is set to renew in one week. If they decide not to insure us, we won't have time to find another carrier so quickly. I have shopped around, and the rates are horrible right now. Our best bet is to stay with them."

"Could you email me a copy of the letter and any other communication you have had with this company regarding the policy renewal and inspection?" Alex asked, handing him his business card. "My email is right there," he pointed to the bottom of the card.

"Sure, sure, I can get that to you tonight," Brian agreed, pocketing the card.

"That would be great. Can we go look at the fire scene now?" Alex gestured in the direction of the charred tree.

"Yep," Brian sprang up from his seat. "Follow me."

He escorted us out the back patio door, through his wide-open grassy lawn, down to what looked to have been a beautiful old spruce tree. How sad for someone to have torched it. Alex looked around, comparing the maps to our location and looking for property lines. Once he was familiar with his surroundings, he unpacked a tiny drone. The drone was a new toy for his PI company. Alex is a private pilot for a growing corporation. Flying is his full-time job, and PI stuff is his side-job. He placed his drone on its takeoff mat. The little guy buzzed to life, hovering over its mat, waiting for Alex to free him. You could hardly see him in the air.

Brian and I stood quietly, watching Alex work. I had never been on a case with him where I wasn't being threatened, and I was fascinated to see how he worked. He had a rhythm, a confidence that complemented his quiet, gentle demeanor. I think I really am dating Batman.

My cell phone buzzed, causing me to jump. I looked at the screen, it was Kandice calling. I texted, 'Call you back in a few minutes'.

She sent back a frowning face and a thumbs-up.

Alex flew his drone around the area, taking pictures from different angles. "You don't have any security cameras on the property, do you?"

"No, but I will be getting them soon. Living in the country like this, we have never needed them, but I guess the world's turning to garbage because even in Podunk, I gotta install cameras," Brian sighed.

We could hear Alex's little drone buzzing as it came in for a landing, parking perfectly on his little landing mat.

"Okay, I think I have everything I need to get started. Please email me those documents we discussed, and I will contact the fire chief to get their report."

Brian escorted us back to the truck. We said goodbye. Once in the truck, I called Kandice, and Alex drove us home.

"What were you doing back out in the valley?" she asked, her tone was not her typical fun-loving Kandice.

"I rode along with Alex," I replied cautiously.

"I thought you didn't bring cupcakes to someone else's party!" she snipped.

"Kandice, it's not like that, I promise. I didn't do anything but watch Alex work." I adjusted the heater vent to give me a little more warmth.

"Taryn, in all my years of being your friend; we have never chosen a boy over each other. That's like if one of the angels had a thing for Charlie and did private missions."

I rolled my eyes. "The angels did do private missions for Charlie sometimes, but that is not what this is, I promise."

"Yeah, and it caused tension between them! Moral of the story: do not investigate without me!"

"Kandice, I am not. We have been friends forever, and I want it to stay that way. I don't keep secrets from you. I rode along with Alex."

"Tell her I will find something she can do to help, but she needs to follow my rules," Alex interjected, having heard my side of the conversation.

"Alex says you can help him if you follow his rules. He can call you in the morning."

"I will think about it. I want to investigate with you. We are good at this," she whined.

"We are okay at this. Look, we just got home, and we are heading to Mom's for dinner in half an hour. I will call you in the morning, I promise. Love you."

"Fine, I love you too."

We disconnected, and I blew out a sigh.

"That sounded fun," Alex smiled.

"That had better be sarcasm," I gently smacked him in the shoulder. "My cupcake analogy came back to bite me in the butt." I wrinkled my nose.

Alex burst out laughing, "You two fight like siblings. She'll get over it. You love each other too much for this to be the thing that ruins your relationship." He patted my hand.

"I know, but I do feel bad. She was so excited earlier, and now she thinks I am deliberately leaving her out."

"Have coffee with her tomorrow, and maybe make your pecan rolls. She'll be over it." Alex replied.

"Are you using my fight with Kandice to get pecan rolls?" I eyed Alex.

"Maybe?" He smiled at her. "Brian Martin mentioned them today, and I thought there's no one who makes better pecan rolls than you."

"Now you are buttering me up to get them. You are a scoundrel. Plus, I know my mom's the one who makes the best. I am a close second."

Chapter 4

We took Alex's Jeep down to my parents' this time. He had graciously backed my truck into the garage for the night so I wouldn't have to deal with a freezing truck in the morning. Alex parked us right out front, came around to open my door, and escorted me up the three steps to the covered porch of my parents' home. A two-story 1800s Victorian, painted cream with blue trim, with a porch swing rocking lazily in the breeze. The large carved mahogany door swung open before we could even knock, and my brother Scotan, *Scotty* to everyone who'd known him longer than five minutes, stood there grinning.

"Alex." He shook his hand, bringing him in for a half-hug.

He turned to me, and I braced myself for impact. Scotty thinks it's a good idea to bear hug me, lifting me off the ground, and sometimes spinning me every time he sees me. He's 6' 4", and I am 5' 5"; he's a lean, muscled firefighter, and I am petite. I guess that means I can be bullied by him.

I coughed as he set me down.

"It's good to see you," he said.

"It's good to see you too." I wheezed, following him into the house.

My family is noisy, and I could hear them talking and laughing before I even stepped over the threshold. It brought a smile to my face.

"That's a bunch of malarkey!" Gramma shouted.

"Gramma's fired up about the city council trying to require residents to remove all bushes and shrubs touching homes to keep insurance companies happy," Scotty warned.

"They can't do that, can they? Gramma's roses have been here for three generations. Her grandma planted them!" I could feel the same rage I heard coming from my gramma brewing in me, faster than a powder keg would ignite. Alex must have sensed it because he placed his calming hand on my shoulder.

"It would take a lot for them to force this on the community. Plus, this is the historic district; there's a whole other set of rules for this area," Scotty replied.

"You are a firefighter, is this necessary?" I asked.

"Anytime there's less to burn, the better, but houses are full of combustibles. A few garden bushes aren't going to stop anything," he replied, taking mine and Alex's coats and hanging them on the little coat rack in the tearoom.

"Were you at the fire by Trestle Bridge this morning?" I asked.

"Yep, initial report thinks it was lightning. We saved the house, but not before one of the bedrooms was lost," Scotty replied.

"Was everyone okay?" I asked, hoping to hear they were.

"Yes, luckily it was a retired couple without pets. They got out just fine."

"Were you on a call last week at the Martins' property just off County Road 253, close to there?" Alex asked.

"I was, that one is still under investigation. Some oak brush and a large pine tree burned. Luckily, the house did not catch fire. There isn't much damage, just the tree."

"What are you three yammering about out here?" Gramma came buzzing around the corner with her hands on her hips.

Somehow her tiny frame filled the doorway. Her fiery red hair was slightly a mess, and the few silver strands she did have seemed to glow.

"Hi, Gramma," I said, giving her a hug. "You won't lose your gramma's rose bushes."

"You bet I won't! I'll be heading to the next meeting," she huffed. "And we are going to invite Margery, the president of the historic district, over for tea. She and I go way back, and her husband was the commander of the VFW a few seats before your father. I got a plan!"

she declared. "Now get your butts in here, I am starving, and I have missed you." She kissed my cheek and reached out for Alex.

"Hey, what about me?" Scotty asked.

She waved him off. "I see you all the time." She smiled.

Alex leaned in and kissed her cheek. Giving her a hug, he said, "It's nice to see you again."

Her green eyes sparkled as she stared at him. She grabbed both our hands and led us through the tearoom into the living room/ dining room area. My mother had already set the table.

Letting go of Gramma's hand, I went to the kitchen to help my mom. She was finishing up seasoning the Stobhach Gaelach (Irish stew).

"Hi, Mom. What can I help with?" I asked, giving her a hug.

"Start slicing the bread, please." She gave the soup one last stir.

Washing my hands, I went to work slicing the bread and arranging it on the wooden serving tray she had placed beside me.

"Gramma's upset over this insurance and code disaster," I commented.

"Everyone is, it's completely uncalled for. But I don't think they can make her remove the rose bushes." My mother sighed. "The cost of living is already too high; this is going to make things worse." My mother looked distressed. "Enough about this drama." She waved her hand, brushing it off. "Let's go enjoy dinner." She grabbed the soup pot, and I followed her with the bread tray and butter dish.

Gramma had corralled my dad and grandpa to the table along with Scotty and Alex. Placing the food in the center of the table, my gramma lit the candles, and we said our meal prayer. Dinner played out like every other family dinner at my house. Lots of embellished stories, laughter, and wine. We didn't play cards tonight, that was a requirement for Sunday dinner, but since it was a Wednesday, weekday dinners are a bit shorter.

I wanted to talk to Scotty more about the fires, but I knew Alex would, since one of them was his case. I would get the details from him on the way home. I offered to wash the dishes since Mom and Gramma did all the cooking. They came to the kitchen with me and had a cup of coffee. Sitting at the little breakfast nook, they talked to me while I washed.

"Did you see in the paper this morning that an insurance adjuster was reported missing by his housekeeper?" Gramma asked, sipping her black coffee. "I think he's the same one people have said goes to city council functions and smoozes those guys up. He's probably the reason my bushes are being threatened," she huffed.

"Mom, you do not know that," my mother scolded her.

"Molly, I will not be removing the bushes. I will not be bullied by tyrants, and this council is getting too high and mighty. They need to be knocked down a peg or ten." My gramma's tiny hands were balls of fists.

My mother rolled her eyes, taking a sip of her coffee.

"Have you guys heard anything about the fires in the valley?" I asked, changing the subject, although I was beginning to think they might be connected.

"It's more malarkey," Gramma said.

"How so?" I asked, rinsing the last soapy dish and placing it on the drying mat.

"Our family has lived in this valley since there was a town to be lived in. The fire seasons haven't changed; just more greedy people. I grew up with the Smuckers. For them to sell that farm to that big company, something's not right out there," Gramma answered.

"It does seem coincidental," I agreed.

My mother yawned, which made us all yawn.

"Well, I guess Alex and I should get going," I said, hugging each of them before going to find Alex.

All of the guys were hanging out in the living room, talking.

Alex glanced at his watch. "It looks like it's time to go," he said.

"Good night, everyone!" I quickly hugged them all goodbye.

We stopped for a moment on my mom's front porch. Alex placed his hands on either side of my face, squeezing it gently. His fingertips ran through my hair.

"I love you, you know that?" he said quietly.

"I love you too." I reached up, cupping one of his hands in mine.

He pulled me in for a long kiss. Releasing me, we gazed into each other's eyes for a moment longer before turning to run to the jeep. The rain was starting to pick up again.

Alex opened the Jeep door for me, closing it after I was settled in.

"Did Scotty have anything to say about the fires?" I asked as Alex pulled out of the parking spot.

"Nothing exciting, just that he was on both calls. The crew agrees things don't appear normal, but they have seen some strange stuff before. The fire inspector will have the final say on the cause of both fires. I will request a copy of that report as well. Maybe we can see a similarity between the two," he answered.

"Gramma's really upset about her rose bushes, and Mom's worried about what all of this is going to cost the working class," I said.

"They're right to be upset, but they have of couple of ideas to keep those bushes. Insurance rates are a whole other ball game. There is not much you can do about what they charge. You are at the mercy of the companies and the legislatures," Alex replied.

The windshield wipers squeaked across the glass, pushing the rain out of sight. I stared at them, finding myself irritated with insurance companies. At least the drive home was a quick one. I was ready to call it a night.

Chapter 5

Giselle, my unofficial alarm clock, went off at 6 am. She would not stop meowing and poking me until I got up. This is a new habit for her, and I have no idea why she formed it. It's annoying. Plus, I am still confused about how she can tell time. I wrapped myself in my bathrobe and started down my short hallway. Giselle led the way, zigzagging in front of me, making it impossible to move at a normal pace without kicking her.

She made her way to her little food table next to the pellet stove. She likes it when you pet her while she is eating. I patted her on the head a few times, turned the pellet stove on, and went to make coffee. It was still dark and a little too early for me to go on my daily run. It was too early for everyone, so I went to my office to get a little work done. Giselle followed me, climbed into her hammock beside my desk, and went to sleep.

I poked her, "I should annoy you now. You woke me up just to go back to sleep." I patted her head and roughed her fur up just a little bit. She was cute even if she had devil moments.

I wrapped my hands around the mug, drew it close, and inhaled the wonderful coffee aroma before sipping. This summer, I had company picnics, several weddings, Memorial Day parties, and even a few wakes to plan. It was shaping up to be my busiest season. Thank goodness no one cared that at a couple of past events I'd planned, someone ended up dead.

Weddings are my favorite to plan, but they take the most work. Glancing at my marked-up calendar, I saw a few days here and there I could use for camping, unless Alex got called to fly Dan somewhere, which happens a lot.

I opened the digital planner I have for one of my wedding clients, and I checked the messages and the notes. It looked like they had signed off on everything. I love it when it's that simple. I went over my checklist and timeline, making sure there wasn't anything for me to complete today. I have a master schedule that keeps everything from all my events in one spot as well. But with weddings in particular, you can never be too careful. Things can go wrong quickly.

My phone danced across the desk. Odd, it's a little early for phone calls. I picked up the phone.

"Hello."

Sniffling came from the other end of the line. "Hello? Are you okay?" I asked as panic started to set in. "Who is this?"

More sniffling came before a struggling voice finally said. "There's a fire."

"Where are you? Have you called the fire department?"

"They're here, but Ryan's gone."

"Rosie, is that you?" I asked.

"Mm hmm. It's me. I didn't know who else to call."

I turned on the local news station to see if there was any coverage on this fire. The mountainside was engulfed in flames. Reports were saying that the fire was only 5% contained.

"Rosie, how close are you to the fire? Where did it start?"

"I don't know. We got an evacuation notice early this morning. Everyone on County Road 253 did. The firetrucks came down the road, announcing it was time to get out. I think the fire is behind us and on the mountain, not in the valley. But it's hard to tell. The smoke is thick." Rosie's voice had begun to steady.

"How do you know Ryan is gone?" I asked.

"He didn't check in at the shelter, he wasn't at his house, and he is not answering his phone."

"Rosie, let me make a few calls, and I will call you back. Are you at the fairgrounds shelter?"

"Yes." She sniffed.

"Good, stay there and stay safe. I will call you back," I reassured her.

The news was playing on a loop, with no new information. The fire started around 3 am. Evacuations were ordered at 5 am. Rosie was right; it was on the mountainside away from houses and heading into the national forest for now. I called my mom. She would be up, and she would know if Scotty got called into work this time.

"Good Morning, Mom."

"Morning, have you heard the terrible news?" she asked.

"Yes, that's why I am calling you. Did Scotty get called out?"

"Yes, say a prayer and ask St. Florian to keep him and the others safe."

"I will. Do you know anything else? The news isn't updating information."

"No, that's all I have heard, too."

"Okay, well, I have another phone call to make. I love you, and I will call you later."

"Taryn, whatever you are up to, be careful, please."

"I will, Mom. I am just checking on friends who live out there."

"Okay, love you, honey."

"Love you too, Mom." I disconnected the phone and looked at Giselle, who was still tightly balled up in her hammock, sleeping.

I heard movement in the hall. Alex must be up. We don't technically live together, he just spends a lot of time here. He appeared in the doorway, wearing only his lounge shorts.

"The Martins called me. They have been evacuated," he said.

"Rosie called me. Ryan is missing."

"What do we know so far?" Alex asked, turning to watch the TV.

"Not a lot. They keep replaying the news blurb. But I called Mom, and Scotty's out there." Saying it aloud made my chest swell. I know that it's his job, but this felt scarier than other times for some reason. Alex must have sensed my distress because he moved towards me, pulled me from my desk chair, and hugged me tightly. I buried my face in his warm, bare chest. Taking a few deep breaths and asking for St. Florian's protection. I calmed, relaxing into his embrace for a few moments.

Pulling away from him, I looked into his honey-colored eyes. "Thank you," I said. "You always seem to know when I need something."

"Call it my Spidey sense." He smiled.

"Ha ha, but Spiderman doesn't do it for me." It's probably because of my innate fear of bugs.

"Noted. Spider-Man, not so good. I know you are worried about your brother and Ryan."

"I am, but we don't know anything yet, so I will do my best to remain calm." I smiled.

"No sudden urges to clean," Alex joked.

"I only clean like that out of anger, not worry. You know this." I rolled my eyes and playfully pushed him. My mom unleashes chemical warfare on their poor house when she is worried or overly stressed.

"It made you smile." He leaned in and kissed me before leaving to get a cup of coffee.

I peered out the window towards the burning mountainside. There was an eerie glow illuminating the mountain's silhouette. The sun was starting to peek over the mountaintops, and someone was coming up the steps to my house. Giselle must have sensed it because she jumped off her hammock, sending it rocking, and ran over to the window, pushing back the sheer curtain to see who it was.

"Alex," I hollered, "Someone is coming up the steps."

The knock came, and we went to answer it together. Standing on the other side of the door was Robert, pillow tucked under his arm and a duffel bag slung over his shoulder.

"Honey, I'm home!" he sang out.

Alex looked at me and shrugged his shoulders. "He's your stray."

"Robert, what are you doing?" I asked, letting him into the house and closing the door behind him.

"I have been evacuated. I was told to take shelter at the fairgrounds or at a friend's. I checked in at the fairgrounds so they would know I wasn't still at large, but decided we are friends and I want to stay with you."

I sighed. How does this happen to me? Robert is my ex-fiancé, and every time I turn around, we are roommates.

"Why am I the friend you chose to stay with?" I asked, following him to the couch.

"Because, why not? We are familiar. We know each other's idiosyncrasies, and I wanted to." He smirked, looking towards Alex, who had taken a seat at the dining room table. Alex waved back, looking unamused.

I didn't even get a chance to reply when there was another knock at the door. "What is this? I am not a shelter!" I returned to the door and proceeded to open it when Kandice waltzed in.

She scanned the room. "Oh, look, the gang's all here."

"I knew you liked hanging out with me!" Robert grinned and winked at Kandice.

"Like, may be too strong a word, Robert. I would say tolerate is more like it," she said sweetly.

Alex choked on his coffee. Making Kandice smile. "He agrees with me." She nodded in Alex's direction.

"Alex, will you make more coffee? I am going to need it. I have a headache starting to form," I said, rubbing my temples.

"You may want to put a shirt on, too. Since we have company." Robert added.

"If you're talking about me. Leave the shirt off. I like a sexy distraction." Kandice smirked.

"Well, in that case..." Robert started to pull off his shirt.

"Stop!" I shouted. "I love you all! But it is way too early in the morning for this. I haven't even gotten to run. Robert, keep your shirt on."

"Honey, you are not running outside today. The whole town is filling with smoke," Kandice replied.

"I have a question." Robert stood up.

"Your shirt stays on because I want it to," I answered.

"Fine!" he groaned, sitting back down on the couch.

"Honestly, Taryn, it's not like he is bad to look at. Actually.."

"No, Kandice!" I interrupted her.

"We are all adults, let's act like it, please. Now, what do you want for breakfast? Pancakes or coffee cake?" I asked.

"I vote coffee cake," Alex said while filling the coffee pot.

"Coffee cake it is!" I announced.

"We didn't get a vote," Robert complained.

"That's what happens when you're not the boyfriend anymore," Kandice retaliated. "Good choice, Alex."

I rubbed my temples. Alex wrapped his arm around, and whispered, "We could ditch them and go to my place."

"It would never work; they're like bloodhounds. There is no escaping."

I poured everyone their first round of coffee and passed them out. "We have work to do. While I am making your cake, I need you guys to find out where Ryan may have gone. Robert, see if he checked in at the checkpoint, if you can. Kandice, start looking into where the evacuees are asked to go. We know the fairgrounds, but are there others opening up?" I barked out orders. If this group wants to team up, they need a commander at the helm.

"Alex, can you call Rosie back and see if she has heard anything? I am sure she will be thrilled to hear from you." I rolled my eyes.

Alex chuckled and grabbed my phone, while I went to whip up a coffee cake. Forty-five minutes later, the cake was coming out of the oven. We still had no idea where Ryan was, and the fire was still only 5% contained. The news kept replaying the aerial footage of the glowing fire. It was so dark when they took the footage that all you could see was the orange flames against the faint black outline of the mountain.

"Mmm…," Kandice moaned. "Why are you such a good cook?"

"Don't flatter her too much, she'll get a big head," Robert added.

"I already know I am a good cook. My head can't get any bigger." I smirked, "But I am glad you all are enjoying it."

"It's perfect, babe," Alex said, swallowing a bite of gooey coffee cake.

"What do you know about that case?" Kandice asked, shoveling another scoop of cake into her mouth.

"Not much, he hasn't had any time to do any-thing with it," I said, sipping my coffee, trying to savor it with the coffee cake. Instead of inhaling it like Robert. Who was on his way to get a second piece.

"Actually, I did discover that the insurance company the Martins use has had a lot of com-plaints filed against it for denying claims. One report I found has the denials at a 71% rate," Alex replied, taking another bite of cake. "That might explain why they are trying to drop some of their existing homeowners."

"You weren't wrong. You do a lot of paper trail digging," I said.

"Yep, not a lot of hanging out in black cloth-ing and stalking people." Alex grinned.

"Where's the fun in that?" Kandice com-plained.

"You all need to get a life. You should come out with me sometime. The only black clothing we will be wearing will be for black-tie events, and of course, Taryn, you can wear the black lingerie afterwards." Robert winked at me.

I rolled my eyes. "Thanks for the charming offer, but no."

"What kind of lingerie are we talking about?" Kandice asked

"Don't encourage him." I jabbed Kandice in the ribs.

The banter between those two continued after breakfast, but they cleaned the kitchen for me, so that was nice.

It was 10 am, and the last three hours of our lives had been spent glued to the TV, hoping for news updates. Social media was providing better information than the news stations. Several of the Silver Springs community pages had been posting updates on shelters, missing animals, and missing persons. This was turning into a horrible nightmare for our little town. The suspicion rose as several posts claimed arson as the cause. Who would do such a thing? Fires are so unpredictable and dangerous. It appeared as though the fire may have grown to twenty acres and was heading east, away from Silver Springs, for now. The rain had started back up again, which was a blessing since it cleared the air of most of the smoke and it helped the firefighters out.

My phone buzzed; it was Rosie again. "Hello, this is Taryn."

"Have you heard anything? Ryan still hasn't checked into the shelter." Rosie sounded worried.

"No, I have tried calling him. I have called friends, but I have not heard from him."

"What do we do?" Rosie asked.

Kandice motioned to me that she was heading out. She had class to get to. She was in school to become a dental hygienist. I waved goodbye.

"I am not sure, but the fire isn't at the campground. He is probably just fine. I will call you the moment I hear something," I said, trying to reassure her before we disconnected.

I liked Ryan a lot. He was a retired Army officer, never married. He purchased the campground years ago, and I worked there a couple of summers in high school. He was always kind and helped out the community, but he flew solo most of the time. I never saw him date anyone.

Robert had made himself comfortable on my couch, and Alex was on the little couch in my office, working on his laptop.

"Robert, we have work to do, so we'll be in the office if you need anything," I said, more out of kindness than really wanting to do anything for him.

"'Work', right," he said, winking.

"Not everything is sex, Robert." I rolled my eyes and left.

We worked on various projects for the remainder of the day, with Robert giving us updates on the fire, which wasn't much.

Chapter 6

Kandice was sitting in her Jeep out front, waiting for me. My stomach turned. I have both Alex and Robert in my house. Sneaking out wasn't going to be easy. I felt guilty about it, too. If something bad happens again, they aren't necessarily going to be able to save me.

Maybe I should tell them what I am doing? They would disapprove; heck, I would disapprove, too. And if it weren't for my friendship with Ryan, I wouldn't be doing this.

Sneaking to my office, I wrote a note and left it on the kitchen counter next to the coffee pot. It read, *I got a phone call from Ryan asking for some help. Kandice and I are going to see him. I have my phone with me. Love you boys, XOXO, Taryn.*

I hadn't noticed Giselle behind me, and as I turned around, I tripped over her. She let out a yowl and took off running.

"I'm so sorry, baby," I whispered, but she was gone.

Robert started rustling on the couch. I ducked down, hoping not to be seen. A moment later, I could hear him lightly snoring. I crept to the front door, carefully unlocking the deadbolt and then the handle, all while holding my breath. I stepped outside, closing the door behind me, taking a deep breath.

The sky had an eerie orange glow. You could see the mountain peaks lit up by the fire. I rushed down the steps to the jeep, looking over my shoulder to see if one of the boys had figured out I'd left. The house appeared to be still.

"What took you so long?" Kandice asked as soon as I opened the jeep's door.

"I had to leave a note."

"A note or a novel? I have been out here for 10 minutes, and you texted *me*," she mocked, while pulling the Jeep away from my home.

I watched it get smaller and smaller until we turned onto Main Street. No lights came on.

"You don't have two men in your house that would not approve of these shenanigans," I said.

"I have Trey." Her tone was sassy.

"He's not here, so that doesn't count." I retaliated.

We approached the lookout point, and I could see Ryan's truck pulled off to the side of the road. There were several other cars parked here. I assumed they were evacuees' cars that they didn't want to leave home. The road was closed to all non-emergency traffic. We parked the

Jeep next to Ryan's truck and got out. Ryan was rummaging in the back seat.

"Just a minute," he hollered. "I am looking for my black clothes."

"Black clothes?" I looked down at myself. I was in jeans and a hoodie.

"Black is best for sneaking around," Kandice said, motioning her hand across her body. She was dressed in all black.

"I know that, but I thought we were going to talk to the gatekeeper," I said.

"Nope, already tried that. They won't let anyone back in, but I know the route to take. I have been coming and going since they tried to kick me out." Ryan's face lit up with a grin.

"Then why do you need us?" I asked.

"Because I found something, and I want you to see it," he said, his tone becoming serious.

"Why not call Detective David Parker?"

"Because something is not right. The fire broke out overnight and has grown to 40 acres, but the compound they have set up is for something much bigger. I have a theory, but need to check it out first."

"There's a compound? What are you talking about?" I asked.

"Here, pull these on over your jeans," he said, tossing a large pair of black sweatpants at me. Barely catching them, I held them up. They had to be twice the size of me.

"If you had dressed appropriately, you wouldn't have to wear them," Kandice scolded.

I narrowed my eyes at her. "Don't," I said, raising a finger.

Kandice grinned. The ground was wet and muddy. I had to sit in the Jeep and remove my shoes to pull the pants on. Ryan handed me a large, black rain jacket. After putting it on, I looked like a walking tent.

"Come on, let's get this over with," I groaned.

"This way. Follow me," Ryan pulled back the branches of a thick oak bush. There was a little path I would never have seen. We lined up in single file and crept down the path. I slipped and almost fell a couple of times. The path wound down into the valley, taking us along the river. I could see vehicle lights coming and going on the road above us. The smoke was thick; it made my eyes and throat burn. Noise from the machinery muffled any sound we may have made.

Ryan held up his hand, motioning us to stop. We froze, holding still and listening. After a few moments, we got the signal to continue. The path led right into the campground, but to my surprise, the camp was full of military personnel. They had created a tiny city in less than 24 hours.

"I am gonna kill him!" Kandice whispered.

"What? Who are you going to kill and why?" I asked.

"Look." She pointed towards the trailer with satellites pointing in all directions. "Trey!"

"Oh my gosh! What's he doing here? I thought he was out of town again?"

"That's what he told me." Kandice started to head towards him. I quickly yanked her back down into the bushes.

"What's the hold-up?" Ryan crept back to us.

"We discovered that Kandice's boyfriend is working with these guys." I pointed in Trey's direction.

"He's a hired hand, not military. Don't worry about it." Ryan brushed the news off like it was nothing. "We need to keep moving."

I didn't care for Ryan's lack of empathy. In fact, I was starting to get annoyed.

"We will figure out why Trey is here," I reassured Kandice.

Ryan motioned for us to follow him.

"Come on, before he gets impatient," I said.

"No, I want to see what he's doing," Kandice insisted.

I couldn't blame her; I would want the same thing if it were Alex.

"Ryan, we will continue later. We are watching from here first," I said.

"Do whatever you want, but I'm going," he said gruffly and stormed off.

Kandice and I stood quietly watching the camp's movements. It looked like they were setting up weather-tracking devices. I knew that large fires can create their own weather, but 40 acres hardly seemed big enough for this type of setup. They must be planning on it growing before they get it under control.

"Why wouldn't he tell me he was in town?" Kandice asked.

"He's probably not allowed to. He hasn't been allowed to tell you where he goes in the past. You've always known he did some sort of government freelance work," I said, reassuring her that this was normal for his job.

"That's no excuse. This is my home, my life. He should have said he was in town," Kandice scoffed.

I patted her shoulder, "Don't hold it against him too long. Let him explain first."

"Maybe," she grumbled.

"Let's go see if we can find Ryan and whatever it is he wants us to see."

"This looks like the compound to me," she protested.

"It looks like a government weather station." I pulled at her. Reluctantly, she followed my lead, and down the slippery, muddy path we went.

The smoke seemed to thin as we approached the campground entrance and office. There were more military personnel and a massive motor coach set up. Men stood guard at the front door. There was little movement, and I couldn't see Ryan anywhere.

"Maybe this is what he wanted me to see? They have taken over the campground and his office. I wonder who is inside the motor coach?"

"Someone or something worth guarding," Kandice replied.

"Let's keep going. Ryan's house isn't far. He owns the property adjacent to the campground." I pointed further down the path. We had barely got to the clearing before an all too familiar crime scene appeared.

I froze, causing Kandice to run into the back of me. A man lay face up in the mud. His body was just off the path. My stomach started to swirl. My guess was he's dead.

Kandice stepped around me. "And now we have a real case!" she announced, way too enthusiastically.

"This is what I get for sneaking around in black clothes." I blew out a sigh.

Realizing that this had become my life, and that I was getting way too comfortable with dead people, I took a moment to reevaluate my life choices. Kandice, on the other hand, wasn't only comfortable, she was ready to investigate.

"This is the first time you have ever encountered a dead body, and it doesn't bother you?" I asked.

"No, why should it? This isn't the first murder we have solved."

"I threw up the first time I saw a body, and we haven't solved this murder yet."

"Oh, but we will." Kandice smiled.

I pulled out my phone and dialed Detective Parker.

"Do you know what time it is?" he said, answering the phone.

"Yes, but I bet you know why I am calling you at this time." I grimaced.

"What have you done now?" he asked.

"Nothing, I swear," I protested. "But I have found a body, and I think it's the missing insurance adjuster, but I can't be for sure."

"Where are you?"

"Well, it's complicated."

"Everything with you is complicated," he groaned.

"Kandice, don't," I said, as she poked the body with the toe of her shoe.

"What? I need to be sure he is really dead," she explained.

"I am pretty sure the gash in him gives that clue away," I said sarcastically.

"Taryn, where are you so I can come down?" David Parker asked.

"I'm...." My phone beeped, and the service died.

"Great, my cell service is gone."

Kandice pulled her phone out to check. Hers was gone too. I snapped a picture of the body.

"Let's hike back up to where we have service again."

Only one guard was out in front of the motor coach. There was no one else around. We kept up the trail until we approached the weather station encampment. Pausing a moment, we searched for Trey. He was hard to spot at first. I heard the familiar hum of a drone. I looked into the sky, but couldn't see anything. Moments later, I could see the large drone preparing for takeoff. The personnel had cleared away from its launch pad. This drone was huge; a small dog could fit into it. Alex's drone fits in the palm of your hand.

Startled, I jumped at Ryan's hand on my shoulder.

"We've got to move now! That drone has infrared tracking, they will see us," he hissed.

We hustled out of there, scrambling to run back up the path without slipping or breaking an ankle. I tried to listen for the drone, but it was too hard to hear anything over our sloppy footsteps and the engine noises.

"Where did you go while we watched Trey?" I asked once we were back at the lookout point.

"I went to my office. That's where their headquarters is set up. You just saw the base camp. I heard them arguing about the mess that was created and how they have to spin this in their favor."

"Is that blood on your hand and cheek?" I asked, pointing to the dried red streaks across his face.

"Oh, this. I scratched myself on the oak brush." He waved me off, like it was nothing.

"Must have been a big scratch," Kandice huffed.

Ryan glared at her. I had never seen him look so angry. Something felt off, but I didn't want to press the issue.

"Did you at least find what you were looking for?" I asked, changing the subject.

"No, let's come back tomorrow night," Ryan suggested.

Eyeing him suspiciously, "We will try. Where are you going now?" I asked.

"I don't know yet. I need to lie low for a while," he replied.

I slipped out of the clothes he had given me to wear and handed them to him now that we were back at our cars.

"I am moving the event to the backup weekend. There is no way we are having a reopening event this weekend," I said.

"Probably for the best," he replied, accepting the bundle of damp clothes.

My cell buzzed back to life, and I had five missed calls from David. Pocketing the phone, I said goodbye to Ryan. Kandice and I got into the jeep.

"You didn't tell him about the body?" Kandice questioned me.

"I don't know why I didn't. It just didn't feel right," I said, surprised at the words coming out of my mouth.

My cell buzzed again. "Crap, it's Alex."

Kandice giggled. "It was only a matter of time."

"Take us home. I need to call Alex now so he doesn't send out a search party and then fill in David."

Chapter 7

The lights were on when we pulled up to my house. I sat there for a minute, contemplating the angle in which I wanted to play defense, knowing full well both boys and Detective Parker were unhappy with my adventures.

"What are you doing?" Kandice asked.

"Trying to find enough glitter to bedazzle my story so the boys don't murder me." I sighed.

"You'll be fine, they'll get over it. It's not like they haven't done things that turned out differently according to plans."

"Oh, I know." I blew out a sigh. "Here we go again," I said, wrenching open the door. Kandice didn't move.

"What are you doing? You're coming in," I said, still partially in the Jeep.

"No way, you're on your own with those guys. Plus, I have to figure out what I am going to do with Trey."

"Nope, you are coming in there with me. It's part of the Angel package. We will take this as a team," I demanded.

Kandice fidgeted with the steering wheel. I could tell she was contemplating ditching me the moment both my feet were on the ground. I stared at her. I was not backing down.

"Fine." She shut the engine off and stepped out of the Jeep.

We climbed the steps to the front door. It was two in the morning. Alex opened the door with Robert on his heels. Neither one of them looked happy. Their faces a mix of anger and relief to see we were fine.

"What were you thinking? How could you sneak out in the middle of the night and go to the evacuation zone? What if you had been trapped in the fire?" Alex rattled off questions.

Before I could answer, Robert started in. "Why didn't you tell us? This was your fault, Kandice. You're a bad influence. Who's the dead guy?" he demanded.

I had a headache forming. "We need coffee before I answer any of your questions."

"If anyone's a bad influence, it's you, Robert." Kandice pointed out.

Alex knew I would want coffee and had it ready. As I was pouring a cup, he wrapped his arms around me. "I am just glad you are safe. My stress levels have risen since dating you. I can't protect you if I am not there to do the protecting."

"I know, that's why I left a note. The body wasn't part of the plan." I half smiled.

"It never is." He kissed me on the top of my head before leading me to the dining room table.

Robert rushed me, nearly spilling my coffee, he shoved Alex out and hugged me, kissing me on the cheek. "This is why I chose to stay with you." He smiled.

Gently pushing him away, I took a seat.

"It doesn't look like it took much glitter," Kandice huffed.

"We will figure out what's going on with Trey. I am sure everything is fine. He is a good man," Alex tried reassuring her.

Just as we all got settled with our coffees, Detective Parker was at the door. Alex greeted him and let him in. David scanned the room. "Looks like *Mystery Inc.* is at it again," he said in a very unamused tone.

"That's a new one. I call Fred," Robert piped up.

"No way are YOU Fred," Kandice argued.

"It was a metaphor," David said, taking a seat.

He pulled out his notebook, took a chair at the table, and began his interrogation. I explained why we were out there and what we had found.

"Did you touch or move the body?" he asked.

"No, but Kandice poked it with her foot." David grimaced, as I said it.

"I wanted to be sure he was dead." She defended her actions.

"Here." I handed him my phone. "I took a picture when the cell service dropped."

"This is disturbing. Who else was around when you found the body?" he asked, taking my phone and inspecting the picture.

"No one, just us. Up the path a little way is the motorcoach and the guard, but we didn't see anyone and no one saw us," I answered.

"I have a call in to incident control. Once they confirm it's a death investigation, I'll get escorted in. Alex, can you join me?" He handed my phone back to me.

"Yeah, let me go get dressed," Alex replied. He headed down the hall to change.

"We want to join you!" Kandice protested.

"Alex can join me for two reasons: he is on the reserve and his investigation may involve the victim. You can not." David shut her down immediately.

Kandice huffed, crossing her arms across her chest and leaning back in her chair. "You won't know where to find the body." she shot back smugly.

David rubbed his temples. "Fine, you win. You can show me where the victim is. But then it's over for you. Got it?" He sounded annoyed, and his expression mirrored his tone.

Kandice perked up in her chair and grinned.

"Nothings ever over with them. You know that, right?" Robert felt the need to point out.

I glared at him. He wasn't making this any better for us. He just winked at me and grinned.

"It will be this time," David insisted.

Kandice started to say something, then thought better of it. David's phone chirped, he had clearance to enter the emergency zone.

"Alright, let's go. We have an escort waiting for us."

Robert changed clothes in the living room with everyone sitting there. The man knows no shame.

"Sorry, Robert. You can't come." David stopped him.

"Why not? Everyone else get's to," he complained.

"I am not sure I fully understand this group's dynamic, but you weren't at the crime scene, were you?"

"It's complicated," I said.

"No, but I have a vested interest in this," Robert said. "Plus, these guys are my friends. They will need my assistance."

"I could lose my job. This isn't a game," David said.

"You are right, it's not. But I could make a sizeable donation to your department on your behalf." Robert smiled.

"That's bribery, and I *will* lose my job for that."

"It's only bribery if you tell me I must stay here. I will have to make an announcement to the local news station about this."

"And now that's blackmail," David replied.

"You are a stick in the mud. It's all in how you interpret it. See, I choose to see the donation as a gift in the name of a very talented officer, and if I am left behind, it's my civic duty to inform the community if there's a potential threat. Think about how awful it would be if there's a mass murder out there and no one was warned," Robert rambled.

By the time he finished, I think everyone was confused.

"Can he come if he promises to stay in the car?" I asked. I wasn't sure I was happy about leaving him in my house unattended. We have mostly come to terms with our relationship, but not that long ago he was creepily obsessed with me and kept breaking into my house.

"But he won't. None of you do. That's the problem." David sighed.

Alex and David rode in the patrol car while Kandice, Robert, and I were in the Jeep. Ryan's truck was still parked at the lookout point. Following Detective Parker through the checkpoint/ entrance, we waited for our queue to move forward. I could see David talking to the guard. After a few moments, we were allowed through. The escort took us to Ryan's driveway, which was the best place to enter since whatever they were doing at the campground meant that we weren't allowed in. As we passed the campground entrance, there was a sign: Military Personnel Only. It's a lot of fuss over a weather station, I thought.

"They have a big operation going on here," Robert commented.

"Yeah, seems like overkill for a small wildfire," I replied.

Kandice parked the Jeep. Detective Parker motioned for us to get out. He and Alex were talking to our escort. We joined them. The escorts name was Jack, he was still partially dressed in his fire gear. I had met him once before at a fundraiser he and Scotty were part of.

"Taryn, nice to see you again. I'll have to let Scotty know you are here." He smiled.

"Thanks, but I wish it was for something better than a dead body." I half smiled.

"Enough chit-chat," David interrupted. "We need to find the crime scene before it's further disturbed."

"There's a little path along the river. The body was just off the path," I said.

We all marched across Ryan's yard, down to the path, following it back towards the campground. My heart stopped when a loud bomb sound went off. Before I could duck, Alex reached out to grab me, as Robert tackled me, causing us to spin out of control, hit the ground and slide across the mud.

I moaned. Robert was sprawled out across me. I was covered in mud, and I was pretty sure I was bleeding from somewhere, since my whole body ached.

"Why did you tackle me?" I complained.

"I was saving you," he protested, and attempted to untangle himself from me.

Alex reached his hand out, helping me up.

"What the heck was that?" Kandice asked, straightening herself, dusting bits of twigs and leaves off. She had ducked into the bushes.

"That was a pine tree exploding. The resin in the tree can heat up in an extreme heat zone, causing the tree to explode," Jack answered.

"Scotty, is he okay?" Panic started to creep in.

"He's working the medic bay right now, so it's unlikely he was near the explosion."

I felt my heart slow at his words. "Thank you, St. Florien," I whispered.

"Babe, you are covered head to toe in mud. Are you okay?" Alex asked.

I looked down at myself. I was a sloppy, muddy mess. My hair was caked in mud. I groaned.

"You can not ride in my Jeep like that," Kandice pointed to both Robert and me. Robert was a lot less muddy than me, since I am pretty sure I was the mud blocker for him.

"We have clothes that you both can have," Jack said.

"If you think you're okay to continue, let's get to the body and then I can send you back to get changed," David suggested.

I was cold, aching, and generally unhappy with my current situation. But I agreed, and we trudged forward.

Arriving at the spot where the body was, there was no body.

"I don't understand. He was right here." I pointed to the spot where he had lain.

David pulled out a penlight and shone it across the ground. It lit up with glowing bluish specks. "There is blood here," he said, as he followed the specks to a larger pool. "If I had to guess, the body was moved," David announced.

"Can we follow the speck trail with your pen?" I asked.

"We are going to give it a shot. It's tough with all of this rain," he replied.

Alex pulled out a pen and began shining his light as well.

"Hey, where did you get that?" Kandice asked.

"I keep one on me when I do investigations." Alex smiled.

"We need those," Kandice said, talking directly to me.

All I could think about was how Alex became more like Batman every time we encountered a mystery.

Robert pulled out his phone's flashlight. "This works just as well," he said, pointing to the red drops on the ground.

"Yeah, but it's not as cool," Kandice grumbled.

"Why would someone move the body?" I asked, thinking out loud.

"Maybe we interrupted the killer," Kandice said.

That's a thought I didn't want to believe because the killer would know who we are.

"That's what I am worried about," Detective Parker chimed in, still staring at the ground and following blue specks.

"Or, the killer has a helper, and the helper was asked to move the body," Robert suggested

"It is possible. Jack, can you take these guys to get changed? We don't need everyone's footprints trampling the scene." David ushered us in the direction of the cars.

"I'll radio command. I am supposed to stay with you. We don't need anyone getting lost out here," Jack replied.

Jack pressed the button on his radio. "Command, this is Fire Patrol Two. I need an escort and minor medical attention for a couple of civilians. Property adjacent to the KOA Camp in the evacuation zone."

A voice responded, "Fire Patrol Two, copy. Medic unit en route. Advise on patient count."

"Two civilians, minor scrapes. Non-emergent," Jack replied.

"You three, stay there." David directed.

"I didn't fall in the mud. I shouldn't have to stay put," Kandice protested.

"No, but I allowed you to come so you could show me where the body was. Now that you have, the rest of the investigation is for me to take care of."

Kandice's phone rang before she could argue with David. She flashed the screen at me. It was Trey's big, goofy smile.

"Aren't you going to answer it?" I asked.

She stared at the phone until it stopped ringing and went to voicemail.

"Kandice, why didn't you answer it?"

"I don't know."

We stood in awkward silence until lights approached us. The medic unit had arrived. The firefighter approaching us was backlit from the headlights, but I knew that tall figure was my brother. I ran to him.

"Scotty!" I yelled

"Taryn! What are you doing out here? It's dangerous," he scolded.

"Um, nothing really. I..."

"She found another body." Robert approached me from behind. I could feel the warmth of his body against mine.

"Where's Alex?" Scotty asked, eyeing Robert.

"It's nice to see you too," Robert said.

"I'm over here," Alex hollered from down the trail.

"Everything is fine." I assured my brother. I could see relief in his eyes. Scotty hadn't seen Robert since our breakup, and he wasn't sure he liked him being in my life. I can't blame him. Robert and my breakup put me through hell. But I had managed to forgive him. Alex had accepted that he's a part of my life. My family will eventually get there too. Heck, even Kandice has come around. Not long ago she wanted to kick his ass.

I looked over at Kandice. She was still staring at her phone and walking behind us. "Are you alright?" I asked.

"I don't know," she answered again.

Reaching out, I grabbed her hand. "Let's go home, talk to Trey, and get this confusion cleared up." I smiled, pulling her towards Scotty's truck.

"So what happened? You're covered in mud and sticks," Scotty asked as we headed to his medic unit.

"I was protecting her. I heard a loud sound, and I covered her with my body to shield her." Robert stood tall.

"He heard a tree explode and tackled her," Kandice remarked.

Scotty shook his head in disbelief. He set up a portable wash station. I washed my hands and face the best I could. Using a towel, I tried to wipe as much mud out of my hair as possible. Scotty checked me over for injuries. I only have a few scrapes, and bruises were forming.

"Why were you out here?" Scotty asked while cleaning the large scrape I had on my arm.

I winced as he sprayed the antiseptic gel. "Ryan asked me to help him. While we were out here, Kandice and I found a body," I said, looking away from my cut. "Detective Parker needed to know where it was." Turning my head back, my gaze locked onto Scotty's gray eyes.

"Taryn, you can't get involved. You aren't trained for this. You have been lucky in the past." He cleaned the cut on my forehead.

"I.."

Kandice interjected, "But we are good at this."

"Good or not, I don't like it. You two are far more important than some case that Detective Parker can handle," Scotty replied, handing me my change of clothes. "You can change in here." He pointed to the little curtained area.

I held up the gray sweatpants and sweatshirt with the words Silver Springs Fire and Rescue stamped across the front. "Thanks."

Robert had finished washing up and sauntered over. Scotty begrudgingly checked him out as well. Robert only had a couple of small scrapes that did not need medical attention.

Once changed, I hugged my brother goodbye, and the three of us loaded into Kandice's Jeep to go home.

"Hey, Scotty!" I yelled from the jeep's window. "Take care of Alex. Don't let him get hurt in the fire."

"You got it, sis! Love you!" he hollered back.

Chapter 8

"So, what's the plan now?" Robert asked, leaning forward in his seat.

"We let David and Alex find the body, I guess." I shrugged.

Kandice was staring at the road. I don't think she even blinked.

"Hey, you and Trey are going to be okay," I said, reaching over and placing my hand on her.

"I agree, no guy is going to walk away from someone that likes the stuff you do," Robert winked.

"Stop it!" I smacked at him, forcing him to sit back in his seat.

Kandice burst out laughing.

"What?" I asked.

"She knows," Robert smirked.

"How do you know what I do?" Kandice asked, stopping mid-laugh.

Robert sat up straight in his seat, speechless. The look on Robert's face had me and Kandice in stitches. He was still a little worried she would beat him up.

"I am going to drop you guys off and head home," Kandice said as she pulled up to my house. "It's late, or early, however you want to look at it."

"What are you going to do?" I asked, not sure it was a good idea to leave her.

"I am going to bed, but I will be over to have coffee with you before my class starts."

I eyed her suspiciously. She did have class tomorrow. However, with as upset as she is with Trey, I wasn't sure she wouldn't do something a little crazy.

"Don't give me that look. I am going to bed," she insisted.

"Fine, but I don't want you to do something we all will regret. He has been great so far. I know there is an explanation in this. Don't forget, you're the one who pushed me to allow Alex in when things weren't adding up," I scolded.

"What is this? You pushed them together?" Robert piped up. "I was trying so hard to unravel it, and all this time it was you thwarting me." He crossed his arms.

"You did that yourself," we said in unison, causing us to laugh again. I leaned in and hugged her, kissing her on the cheek.

"I love you, dear friend. We will figure all of this out." Smiling, I pulled the handle, opening the door. I stepped out into the hazy night.

Robert following behind me. I waved as my friend drove away.

"You win some, you lose some," Robert grinned.

I punched him in the arm. "Trey is not the kind to lose."

"Hey!" he whined.

Giselle was dancing around the front entryway, meowing when we walked in.

"Hello, sweet kitty," I said, trying to pat her on the head. She kept dodging me. Clearly, she wanted me to follow her. "Alright, what is it that you need?"

She zigzagged in front of me, looking back every other second, making sure I was still following her down the hall. She stopped at her food bowl.

"Oh, no!" I announced. "You can see the bottom of your bowl!" I patted her on the head and refilled her dish. It's catastrophic if she sees even just a peek of the bottom of her bowl. She freaks out, like there is a food shortage. "Silly cat," I said, picking her up and kissing her on the head. She squirmed to get out of my arms and eat.

"You spoil her, you know," Robert said, leaning against the doorframe of my room.

"She is my fur child. What do you expect.?" I pushed past him. "I am taking a shower. No, I don't need your help." I said before he could make a ridiculous comment. "You can have the shower after me." I needed to get the mud out of my hair before I got into bed. I could see he wanted to say something but thought better of it.

"Here," I held up my bag of muddy laundry, "Please toss this in the washer. I'll start the load after you shower.

Taking the bag, he said, "Sorry I tackled you. I really was trying to protect you."

"I know," I smiled. "Thanks."

I let the warm water run over my body, my thoughts racing. Why was that guy murdered and why was his body moved, and how did this connect to the fires? The worst part was where did Ryan fit into this?

Shutting the shower off, I reached for my towel.

My phone buzzed and danced across the bathroom counter. I was still dripping. With the towel in one hand, I reached for the phone. The number flashing on the screen was unknown.

"Hello?"

"Taryn, what have you done?"

"Who is this?" I asked.

"Meet me at the beachside park tomorrow at 2pm." Click, the line went dead.

Weird. I finished drying off and dressed in my warm, fuzzy pajamas.

"The shower is all yours," I let Robert know. "I got a call while I was in there. The number was unknown, the voice male, and he asked me to meet him at the beachside park tomorrow before hanging up on me."

Robert's face twisted in thought with a hint of rage. He wasn't happy, and Alex won't be either.

"I am not showering until Alex is back. I don't trust this and I can't keep you safe from inside the shower."

"It's probably nothing," I said, trying to sound confident. I hadn't done much of anything, and I already had someone upset with me. Talk about bad luck.

"With you, I have learned it's never nothing. Plus, Batman may kill me if something happened to you under my watch." He grinned.

"Surprising, I didn't think you cared what he thought?" I teased.

"I don't really, but you two are very stubborn. And since my attempts to prove my love for you have fallen short, I decided that being your personal bodyguard isn't a bad position to be in." A sly grin spread across his face as he stood up from the couch and closed the gap between us.

"My personal bodyguard?" I rolled my eyes.

"Yes, and it's not a job I take lightly; however, the benefits outweigh the risks." He smirked.

"Robert, I don't know what's going on in your head, but thank you, I think." I wrinkled my nose.

"Let me explain," his grin grew bigger. "I get to stay with you, see you naked, kiss you and protect you. You won't be able to resist...eventually."

"Okay, none of those things are happening. Are you sure you didn't hit your head when you tackled me?"

"Saved you, and no, my head is just fine." He peered at me with his puppy-dog eyes.

"Stop looking at me like that. It makes me uncomfortable," I said, looking away from him.

"What? I am not doing anything," he protested.

"How about this: you can shower with the door open. That way, if I yell for help, you will hear me." I suggested.

"See, it's already working. You want to see me naked." He grinned.

Before I could protest, my phone rang. It was Alex.

"What do you know?" I asked. Covering the phone with my hand, I whispered to Robert, "It's Alex, go shower. I will be fine." I motioned towards the bathroom.

"Not much, the blood trail stopped at the river. We are calling it off until daylight. I will be home soon," Alex said, his voice raspy.

"Okay, be safe, and I love you," I said, hanging up.

I couldn't sleep even though I was exhausted. Noticing the paper sitting on the coffee table, I grabbed it, re-reading the article about the fire season and the one about the missing Reed Jackson.

The fire danger piece wasn't based on any real evidence. It was based on a general western United States assumption that this year's rainfall was going to worsen the previous year's drought conditions. Just ammunition for the insurance companies.

The article about the missing insurance adjuster and city council lobbyist, Reed Jackson, was interesting. A local man was last seen Tuesday morning, the housekeeper reported, and that financial documents were missing.

Who is this housekeeper? I wish I had access to the initial report. Maybe Alex could get it for me. I hadn't noticed Robert had gotten out of the shower. He waltzed through my living room with only a towel wrapped around his waist.

"Forgot these," he bent over his bag and held up his silk boxers.

I looked up from the paper. A bead of water ran down his chiseled abs.

"Like what you see?" he let the towel slip a little lower.

Realizing I was staring, I brought myself back to reality. "Stop it. I know what you are up to. Go get dressed." I shook my head and pointed towards the bathroom.

He grinned and sauntered out of the room.

Good grief, I thought.

The sound of keys at the door made my heart skip. Alex was home. I rushed to the door to let him in. He hardly had a chance to close it before he was kissing me, looking me over. "Are you okay? I didn't get to see you after the medic took you."

"I am fine, just a few scrapes and bruises. Nothing you can't fix for me." I winked at him.

"I am free now." He grinned, picking me up.

Robert cleared his throat, and I rolled my eyes. "We can't. We have a roommate." I frowned.

Alex placed me back down, cutting his eyes towards Robert and grumbled.

"So, you couldn't find the body?" I asked.

"No, the trail went cold once we got to the river. David is bringing in the K9 unit as soon as the sun's up."

"Do we know he is really dead?"

"No, in the picture you took he looks dead, but we have no other evidence other than a blood trail."

"I got a call from an unknown number. The man on the line asked what I had done and wanted to meet at Beachside Park at 2pm." I scrunched my face.

"Not again. You see, this is why I don't want you involved."

"I can't help it. This just happens to me," I protested.

Robert had made himself comfortable on the couch, making a little bed out of it. I looked over at him. He was tucked in, watching us like we were a Netflix episode.

I rolled my eyes. "Show's over. Good night, Robert," I said.

"The show is never over." He winked.

Alex and I went to bed. We had an early morning, and things just kept getting weirder.

Kandice was at my door first thing in the morning. Robert let her in.

"Good morning," she said, waltzing to the kitchen for coffee.

"You look better this morning," I said, hugging her.

"That's because I am! I tossed and turned all night trying to decide what to do with Trey and I figured it out," she smiled.

Robert perched himself on the barstool with his coffee, listening intently to Kandice.

"And what have you come up with?" I asked, taking a seat at the table.

"I am going to investigate Trey!" she said excitedly.

"Why not just call him and ask him what's going on?" I asked.

"And give him a chance to come up with an excuse? I think not. I am going to call him when I am out of class today, lay a few traps, then watch him to see if he is telling the truth." She smiled.

"You are going to sneak back into the camp?" I questioned.

"Well, of course. Ryan is right, there is something else going on out there." Kandice defended.

"I agree completely, but I don't think Trey is the bad guy." I said.

"We will see," she said.

"That might be difficult," I said. "David and Alex couldn't find the body last night. Search and rescue and the K9 unit are going out to see if they can find it. It's going to get really hard to sneak around with all those organizations deployed."

"I am going at night when there won't be as many of them around," she announced.

"Nope, you are not." Alex's voice carried in from the hall. He appeared dressed in jeans, hiking boots, and a flannel shirt. I liked this rugged mountain man look he had going.

Kandice narrowed her eyes at Alex. "You can not tell me what to do." She crossed her arms and leaned back in her chair.

"I am not telling you what to do. I am telling you what you can't do. Trey is my friend, and things aren't what they seem. It wouldn't be right of me not to help keep you out of harm's way. Plus, we are practically family now, and since you have no brothers, think of this as brotherly love," Alex said firmly.

I reached out, placing my hand on hers. "Let's figure this out together. I like your idea of calling him and seeing what he says. Set a trap and see if he falls for it."

"David will be here to pick me up in a couple of minutes. Robert, you are in charge of these two. Keep them out of trouble." Alex ordered.

Robert had been weirdly quiet, perched on his bar stool. He jumped up and saluted Alex. "You got it, boss."

I rolled my eyes. "I think it's funny how you guys switch teams wherever it's convenient for you," I said, staring directly at Robert.

He just grinned.

"I will be back to pick you up for your mystery meeting." Alex said, giving me a quick kiss goodbye.

"Mystery meeting?" Kandice questioned.

"Taryn got a call last night from an unknown number asking her what she had done and wanting to meet her this afternoon," Robert blurted out.

"We haven't done anything?" Kandice murmured, "How could a killer already be upset with you?"

"I don't know. It seems I have a knack for making people mad at me in record time."

"Okay, I gotta go. David's here. Remember, stay safe and don't go on any side adventures." Alex looked directly into my eyes as he warned.

"I have plenty of work to do here this morning. I will see you this afternoon," I said, standing and walking him to the door.

"I love you, you know." Alex's warm hands cupped my face.

"I know." I smiled, leaning in for a kiss. It was a passionate one. The kind that makes you want to leave the world behind. "I love you, too. Be safe out there," I said, closing the door behind him.

"Okay, team, we have work to do," I said, returning to the table. "Kandice, you have to be in class in a little over an hour. Let's call Trey now and see if he answers. Robert, see what you can find out about the fire. Has it progressed? As an evacuee, you may be able to get more information."

"I don't think so. You are not getting rid of me that easily. I was told to keep an eye on you." His smug face begged for me to smack it. He took a seat next to me. Bold, I thought, since he was within punching range.

I narrowed my eyes. "You are not my babysitter, and I wasn't trying to ditch you. Just find out the information." I sighed.

"Cake by the Ocean" played as Kandice's phone flashed Trey's picture.

"Looks like we don't have to call him. Answer it," I urged.

"Hello," Kandice answered.

"I have classes today. What about you? Will you be back in town soon?" She asked as Robert and I stared at her. We were on pins and needles, wanting to hear his side of the conversation.

"Oh, I see. How much longer is the job?" Kandice paused before saying goodbye. She tried to play it off, but her acting skills were lacking today. I was afraid he would see right through her.

"He lied to me. He said he was at a government facility and didn't know how long they would need him. He would try to call me later today after my classes." Kandice's eyes had tears behind them. "This is why I don't get attached," she sighed.

"Kandice, I am telling you. It's going to be all right. I can feel it." It has to be, I thought.

Chapter 9

Kandice had gone to class, and that left me and Robert at my place. I had work to do, moving the grand reopening to the next weekend. Calling all the vendors and performers, I found that most of them would be able to attend next weekend. Only a few had other plans. I had put this information on the original sign-up forms, but not everyone could leave two weekends open. I had prearranged permission to send my food truck vendors to the fairgrounds to serve meals to the evacuees and the fire department. Those poor guys had such long shifts ahead of them. Many of them appreciated my planning. After updating all of the advertising, I let the radio station know the dates had changed so they could start making announcements. I still need to call the newspaper, but I want to ask them questions about the missing insurance adjuster, so I put that off for the moment. Finally, I called Rosie to see if she had talked to Ryan and what she was doing for the campground. Her phone rang several times, and Giselle had decided that walking across my desk and putting her butt in my face was a good idea. I sputtered as I attempted to keep from eating cat hair as her tail whacked me in the face.

"Hello Taryn," Rosie answered.

"Rosie." I coughed. "Just checking in with you. I saw Ryan last night for a few minutes. He said he is lying low for a while." I smacked at my cat, giving her a gentle shove off my desk.

"I talked to him, too. He finally called asking me to cancel all the reservations through this weekend and alert the visitors for next week that they could get cancelled too, depending on this fire," she sighed.

I peered out the window, listening to her talk. The rain had stopped, but the sky was dark and gloomy. "Have you seen him?" I asked.

"No. As far as I know, he hasn't checked into the shelter," she replied.

"Did you know the insurance adjuster, Reed Jackson?" I asked, still staring out the window.

"I met him when he came by the camp several weeks back. He was there to do an assessment on the property before Ryan could renew his policy," she explained.

"Did anything between them seem off?"

"No, only that I didn't like Reed. He kept telling Ryan that he should sell to Camp World and retire. The Camp World Corporation could afford the insurance increases. He was rude, I thought," Rosie explained.

"He was advising on the buyouts?" Interesting, I thought. "Has there been anyone else around who wanted Ryan to sell?" As I asked the question, that stupid woodpecker came out and started to jackhammer my poor tree again.

"I can't think of anybody, but I know an attorney's office had been sending him mail. Whenever he got a letter from them, his face would turn red with anger, and he would storm off to do whatever." Rosie remembered.

Why would he be getting harassed by an attorney? I thought. "Do you happen to remember the firm's name?"

"It was Salgner and Katz," she replied. "Is Ryan in trouble?"

"I don't think so. Alex is working on an arson case that the same adjuster was on. I thought I would ask since it's all in the same area." I half-told the truth. Man, this investigative stuff makes me a liar. I should probably reflect on that.

"If you hear anything else or talk to Ryan, let me know. I have everything moved to next weekend." I said goodbye before she could ask me questions about Alex's case. I probably shouldn't have mentioned that. Giselle had assumed the attack position, squishing her face against the glass and flicking the tip of her tail while not breaking eye contact with the woodpecker.

Robert appeared in the doorway, leaning against the frame. His arms were folded across his chest and feet crossed at the ankles. "The fire is growing," he said, "it's still only 5 percent contained."

"What direction?" I asked, rising from my desk chair.

"It's still heading into the national forest," he replied. "Federal wildland crews are being mobilized."

"At least the town is safe for now," I said.

Robert's phone rang. Answering it, I could hear him say he could be there in 15 minutes.

"Who was that?" I asked.

"Search and Rescue, the sheriff's asking for help with the missing person."

"They called you?"

"Yep, I have been part of the SRA volunteer team for a couple of years now." He smiled. "Now who's your man of mystery?"

"I had no idea," I said, dropping back into my chair.

"There's more to me than you remember." He winked while pivoting and leaving to change clothes. He returned dressed in his hiking gear.

"Okay, I am out. Stay here and stay safe." He kissed me on the top of the head and left. I watched him trot down the steps to his Corvette and drive away. I wasn't sure how I felt about all of this. Now three of the most important men in my life were on a burning mountain. I needed to see my mom. She would know how Scotty was doing, plus her house was close to the newspaper. It is within walking distance, and I wouldn't have to fight for parking downtown. I could park at her place, check in with her and get a little comfort because for some reason I was more worried than I felt I should be.

I could see smoke coming out the front door of my mother's house from a block away. Panic was sinking in. What could have happened? Would they be okay? I parked and ran into the house. "Mom!" I hollered, "Gramma!" It smelled strongly of electrical burning.

"Taryn, we are fine, honey." I heard my mother's reassuring voice coming from the back of the house.

I ran towards them. "What happened?" I asked as my mother and gramma were opening the back door and windows.

"The mopper blew-up," Gramma said.

"It did not blow up. There was an electrical short, and the motor caught fire while I was mopping," my mother explained.

"How is that possible? And why is there so much smoke?"

"The button had been fussy, and your father bypassed the shut-off," my mother explained. "It started smoking, and we didn't notice it until a small burst of flames shot out the side. It burned itself out before we could do much of anything, but not before the house filled with smoke. We are airing everything out and the mopper is on the back porch."

I looked out to the porch. There sat the melted, mangled mopper.

"We usually don't have this much fun cleaning." Gramma laughed.

"Fun? More like terrifying. I am so glad you guys are okay." I rushed my mother for a hug.

"Are you okay?" My mother asked.

Looking up at her, I realized how my mother must have felt every time she thought I was in danger. "Yeah, I was freaked out that something happened to you guys, that's all."

"We are just fine. Probably shouldn't mention this to Margery at tea tomorrow, though. It wouldn't exactly help my campaign against excessive fire mitigation. It's a shame, really. I could've made quite a story out of this.

"Oh, Gramma you will. Just maybe after this whole fire thing blows over." I smiled.

My mother had put on a pot of coffee and pulled out a container of Irish soda muffins. "Sit." She pointed to the little breakfast nook. Gramma and I obeyed, taking our seats. Mom served us muffins and coffee in her shamrock tea set.

"You never need a reason to come by, but why did you come over?" Mom questioned, setting a pitcher of cream and the butter dish on the table.

"I need to go to the Silver Springs Times, and I didn't want to fight the parking. Plus, I wanted to check-in and see if you have heard how Scotty is doing," I said, slathering butter on my muffin. "Last I heard the fire was growing and they are bringing in federal wildland crews."

"Your brother is doing fine," Gramma said, delicately taking a sip of her black coffee. "He told us he patched you up last night." She eyed me.

That snitch, I thought. "I was helping Ryan out, that's all."

My mom stared at me with her bright green eyes. "Is that all?"

Crap, that jerk told them about the body. "Mostly. Detective Parker, Alex, and Robert are all out searching for the missing adjuster," I said, hoping that would be enough information.

My mother tore a small chunk of muffin off and ate it. "I'm glad you are not getting involved. Leave it to those boys."

I looked out the window. Seeing the sad little mopper, I started to laugh.

"I can't believe you killed the mopper." I grinned.

"I did nothing of the sort," my mother huffed. "It's you kid's and your father's fault."

"It might be the aggressive mopping technique you use to de-stress," Gramma piped up, taking a bite of muffin.

My mom frowned, but I appreciated not being the topic of discussion.

We finished our coffee and muffins, and I headed to the newspaper.

The clouds were thick and looming. I had my umbrella in case they burst open. The walk down Third Avenue was beautiful. The Victorian homes stood neatly in a row, like a page out of history. Nothing out of place. Every yard was perfectly groomed. Their spring garden beds overflowed with daffodils, irises, and tulips. I walked the sidewalk, following the picket fences to Second Avenue. Crossing Second, I headed for Main Street. Passing the little shops, many of which had been here since Silver Springs was started.

The town's newspaper is locally owned, family-run, and has been in continuous print since 1808, recording life in the valley long before paved roads, zoning boards, or insurance adjusters came along. The bell jingled as I opened the door to the Silver Springs Times. A small reception desk sat just inside the door. Beyond it, an open bullpen stretched across the room.

We have two full-time journalists for our small paper. Their desks had stacks of back issues, half-marked notepads, and sticky notes everywhere. The air smelled of ink and old paper, and the walls were lined with framed front pages from Silver Springs' biggest news.

I grimaced as my eye caught the Crystal Lakes murder I was involved in last fall.

Racheal Post sat behind the reception desk. I went to school with her. She was a junior journalist. Her long, curly brown hair was pulled back into a high ponytail, slicked back so tight her eyes looked like they were pulled back as well.

"Oh, hey Taryn!" She waved.

"Hi Racheal, I need to update the ads for the KOA grand reopening and the town's summer kick-off. We had to move it to next weekend." I frowned. I still wasn't happy about the rescheduling.

"I thought I would hear from you today. This fire has caused a huge disruption for several of the town's events this weekend. We plan on running a big 2 page update tomorrow morning, and I am updating the website as information comes in." She smiled.

"Thank you so much. Hey, how's the fire coverage going?"

She wrinkled her petite nose. "We are not getting enough updates from incident command. I know search and rescue has been called out, but they aren't saying for whom just yet. We suspect it's the missing adjuster."

"That's actually why I am here, besides the event update."

Her eyes grew wide. "What information do you have?" She grabbed a pen and a pad, hunching over, ready for any tidbit I would give up.

"Well, I was hoping you would give me some information." I smiled.

"Oh," disappointed, she lower her pen and pad back to the desk, straightening herself. "What information are you looking for?"

"Who reported Reed Jackson missing?" I asked.

Racheal peered at me with questioning eyes. "We didn't get a name, but we called the police department to confirm that a missing persons report was filed."

"I was afraid of that. Thanks for your help." I pivoted to leave when Racheal called out.

"Wait." She walked to one of the desks in the bullpen, flipping through a stack of papers. She pulled out a page. "This is the police report." She handed it to me.

I accepted the paper. Looking it over, I noticed the call came from an employee of Suds and Scrubs, a local cleaning company.

"You have had some interesting involvements with murder around here. I assume you think there is something going on." She peered at me.

I could sense the pressure mounting. She gave me something and now she wanted something in return. "I... um..." Crap, I thought, "I am not sure yet, but something is not right with these fires or the adjuster," I replied.

She eyed me, probably thinking I wasn't giving her all of the facts, which I wasn't. "I will let you know if anything comes of this." I offered with a smile.

She frowned but seemed to accept my lack of information.

I exited the newspaper and took a deep breath. The rain had started again. The weather was not behaving according to typical Colorado weather. I popped open my umbrella and headed back to my mom's to retrieve my truck.

Chapter 10

I sat in my truck for a moment thinking about how Suds and Scrubs is connected to this. Was the housekeeper that close to Reed? The paper didn't say who called it in, just that an employee of Suds and Scrubs did. I decided to stop by Suds and Scrubs on my way home. Their office shared the plaza with The Hidden Closet on the north side of town. Taking the short trip up North Main, I parked outside their office, glancing over at The Hidden Closet, the adult store that had been the start of the first murder I was involved in. I shuddered.

Suds and Scrubs was owned by Sheila Weathers, a Blue Star mom, and daughter of Korean war vet Mitch Macaw. I knew them through my Grandpa. He spent so much of his time at the VFW helping veterans that it was hard not to know who our servicemen and women are. They were good people, hard-working people. The shop's window listed its services and phone number. They offered discounted and free cleanings for veterans. A huge sign on the door advertised that you could get your sleeping bags and large comforters washed here. That was new. They weren't a dry cleaner or a laundromat, but they have four industrial super-sized washers and dryers for your extra-large stuff. The little bells on the handle jingled as I opened the door. The washing machines were to the right, and a reception area was to the left. Sheila was behind the desk. She peered over her hot pink reading glasses at me as I entered.

"Taryn, what brings you in?" She smiled, her brown hair was twisted into one of those giant claw clips.

"I was in the area and thought I would stop by to see if you have heard from Ryan. He hasn't checked into the shelter. Rosie called me, worried, and I am too. Since he is a veteran, I figured you may have heard from him," I said, approaching her desk. I actually hoped she had.

"I didn't know he was missing too. I haven't heard from him in a little while," she replied.

"It's nothing official, like Reed Jackson. Rosie and I just haven't heard from him is all."

"Well, Reed Jackson missing is sad, especially now with the fire. He doesn't have any family in the area that I know of, but it's just awful when someone doesn't know where their loved ones are."

"It really is," I said, taking a seat in the reception chair closest to her desk.

"How did you come to know Reed was missing?" I asked, hoping I wasn't too forward.

"Oh, it wasn't me. It was one of my employees. She got us several accounts through Reed, and she noticed he was gone," Sheila replied.

"That's great news for you. I am sure the growth was appreciated. Especially with everything you donate."

"It was a blessing, but I feel bad for her. She is taking Reed being missing very hard. I gave her a few days off. She was very part-time, and usually only worked the new clients she acquired for us, but she was grateful for the break."

"So she was close to Reed. That would explain why she would know about financial things missing." I pushed, knowing I was on the edge and might get shut down.

"I don't know about financial stuff, but they were close from what I could tell." Sheila eyed me. "Taryn, what is this about?" she asked.

"Nothing, really. I am just a little nervous over the fires and Ryan, that's all." I hoped she believed me.

"Oh, honey. How insensitive of me. I didn't think about it from your perspective after everything you have been through. Your Grandpa told me how horrible it was for the family when you were..." She trailed off, like maybe she shouldn't mention that I was kidnapped.

I rescued her, "Sheila, it's okay. I survived." Knowing that I wasn't going to get anything else out of her, I decided to end the awkward conversation.

"Thank you, Sheila." I stood up. "If you do hear anything from Ryan, please let me know."

"Oh, I will, honey. Sorry again." She half-smiled.

"It's fine, really." The door jingled as I exited.

Ella poked her head out of The Hidden Closet. "Taryn!" she hollered and motioned for me to come to her. Ella owns The Hidden Closet. She is an ex-runway model for Victoria's Secret, and in her mid-fifties.

She grabbed me for a tight squeeze. "I haven't seen you much lately, but from what I've heard you have been up to your eyeballs in dead bodies," she said, releasing me.

"More than I want to say, but I am good. Not a lot of bachelor parties to plan lately." I smiled at her.

"You still hanging out with those cutie pies, Robert and Alex?"

"Yeah, things were a little complicated, but for the most part, everything is good now between all of us."

"You know," she gestured to the store, "you don't have to plan a bachelor party to visit the shop." Her hazel eyes peered at me as she smirked.

I blushed, "I know, I will try to stop by more often, but I have a meeting soon and need to go." I leaned in and hugged her again before heading back to my truck.

"You be careful, hon," she hollered.

"I will."

Ella is a sweet woman. A little wild for me, but I love her.

I drove my truck home. The clouds were still gloomy, but no rain.

Giselle was curled up sleeping in her hammock when I entered my office. Petting her soft fur, I looked at the clock. My mystery meeting was in two hours. That didn't give me much time. I needed to see if I could figure out which employee of Suds and Scrubs made the call. Maybe that would lead me to Reed.

I searched Sheila's website. They had several excellent ratings, no surprise there. I noticed the list of companies they service, and Neighborhood Integrity was one of them. Interesting, this would explain the new accounts obtained through Reed. Scrolling further through the website, there was a "Meet the Team" section. I recognized most of these people from around town, but who could have been the one connected to Reed? Stopping on Amy Thompson, she looked familiar, but I couldn't place her. Why did I know that name? I stood and stretched, staring at her photo. I paced my office in thought.

My phone buzzed, startling me.

I jumped; it was Robert.

"Hey, did you find him?" I asked.

"Not yet, but Alex thinks this whole thing is a setup. There's an area we're being quietly discouraged from searching. We have found some igniters that haven't gone off yet."

My grip tightened on the phone. "Are you safe?"

"I think so." His voice sounded strained and a little out of breath. "Listen, I need you to do me a favor."

"Sure," I said. "What is it?"

"Can you call Ryan? I know you two are close, and he is not answering anyone's calls. We really need to talk to him."

"I can try. Why do you need to talk to him?" I asked, worried for some reason.

"I have not talked to Alex or David yet, but most of what we are finding is on Ryan's property. He must know something."

"I see." my stomach turned. "I will try to find him. If I do, what do you want to know?"

"Anything that could help answer the question of where Reed could have gone and what he knows about fire ignition."

"I have to ask you something too. You go to the city council meetings. Who's been leading the rezoning push?"

"Councilman Thompson," he answered. "Why?"

My stomach dropped.

"Because Amy Thompson is his wife, and she works for Suds and Scrubs," I said. "And that company services Reed Jackson. Plus, I've been staring at her picture for five minutes trying to remember why I know her. She has access to properties tied to Neighborhood Integrity, and now to a missing man and an active fire scene," I said.

"Reed was the one pushing Councilman Thompson along, dangling the better life in Silver Springs card in front of him, making him feel like a town hero if he helped to usher in the change," Robert replied.

"This is worse than I thought."

"It looks like you have two people to track down. Be careful with Councilman Thompson. He is a bloated, arrogant ass."

"You be careful out there. I don't like that you, Alex, and Scotty are hiking in a fire.

"We are fine, the smoke sucks, but we are not in the fire."

I knew that, and I could sense he was smiling. We disconnected.

I stared at Amy's picture; she was the newest employee of Suds and Scrubs. She had to be the connection. The rain was steadily beating against my windowpane, and Giselle was still curled into a tight ball in her hammock. I peered out into the mist. My boys were on the side of the fiery mountain, tromping around in the mud and slop, trying to find a body that had seemed to vanish. I wondered just how many people were willing to let this fire burn, as long as it worked in their favor.

Dialing Ryan's number, I waited as it rang. With no answer, I left him a message explaining everything Robert said they had found. I left out the Amy part, just in case something else was going on. I hoped I had not said too much, but I wanted him to call me back, and maybe the information would be tempting enough that he would.

A police car pulled into my driveway. I froze for a moment before realizing the cop was dropping Alex off. I watched as he exited the car and ran up the steps. I raced to the door to let him in.

"Did you find the body?" I asked.

"No," he replied, removing his wet coat and hanging it up.

I frowned. "I talked to Robert. He said he hadn't talked to you or David yet, but that the search and rescue team has been discouraged from searching certain areas, and they have found explosives."

"Yeah, we got that too. David said some attorney requested a 'pause' on the search of certain areas, citing client property rights," Alex replied, grabbing me for a kiss. "It won't last long since we are actively looking for a missing, possibly murdered person, but it's one more thing to delay things."

"Do you think he could be alive?" I asked.

"We really don't know. The amount of blood we found, the temperatures at night, the rain and the fire in that terrain. It's not impossible, but it wouldn't be easy for survival." He walked to the kitchen and filled a glass of water, drinking the entire glass in one swallow. Placing the glass on the counter, he said, "Let me grab a quick snack, and I will take you to meet this mystery caller." He pulled the lunch meat and mayo out of the fridge, making a sandwich.

"Amy Thompson, Councilman Thompson's wife, is probably the housekeeper who reported Reed missing," I said filling Alex in on my morning.

Taking a bite of his sandwich, he groaned, "The zoning guy's wife is mixed up in this? That doesn't look good."

"That's what I thought."

Chapter 11

We drove the short distance to Beachside Park. It was just three blocks north of me and on the riverwalk, the town's paved path that ran the entire distance of Silver Springs along the Winterburn River.

We waited in the truck, watching to see who would show up. I could hear the train's whistle. The tracks were on the other side of the beach. They must have been moving cars out of the fire danger area.

Just as the steam engine passed, a man stepped out of the bushes, dropped his pants, mooned the train, and disappeared back into the brush. Jason, the moonshiner mooner, was back at it, mooning the train.

"What was that?" Alex asked, staring after him.

"How have you lived here almost a year and not know who Jason Moon is?" I laughed. "He's the town mooner. Nearly every day he moons the train, and occasionally, if you're walking down Main Street, he'll moon tourists from his apartment window."

Alex blinked.

"I thought everyone had seen his butt at least once," I said, grinning. "I went to school with him. He's a couple of years older than me."

"Nope," Alex said, shaking his head. "This is new to me."

"David never mentioned our moonshine mooner?" I asked, genuinely surprised. "He's kind of a big deal. It's like hoping you catch a glimpse of Bigfoot when you're in the forest. You haven't really seen Silver Springs until you've been mooned by Jason." I burst out laughing.

Alex started laughing too. "That's ridiculous."

"It is!" I said. "And what's worse is I'm pretty sure there's a map of moon sightings on the town's website."

I wiped my eyes. "He's a legend, and he makes the best moonshine in the area. It's sweet going down, but strong enough to put hair on your chest."

A man in a trench coat, holding a large umbrella appeared on the beach, peering out across the river. He stood at the edge of the water, waiting.

"That must be our mystery caller," I grimaced. Pulling my hood over my head, I jerked at my zipper until it was zipped all the way up.

Alex grabbed my hand, "Listen, no crazy attempts to take on this guy, okay? I won't let go of you this time," he said.

"And I won't ask you to." I smiled.

We got out of the truck and approached the umbrella man. His face was covered with a buff, and he had a baseball cap on, making his gray eyes the only thing I could see.

"Your brother said you found him," he said finally.

My stomach dropped, and I squeezed Alex's hand. "That traveled fast. How do you know my brother?"

"He wasn't just an insurance guy," he said. "He was a pressure point. He was here to bring change."

"You knew him?" I asked.

"He knew me," he corrected. "Showed up at my shop, told me once the corporations moved in, my little moonshine act wouldn't fit the new image of Silver Springs."

My eyes widened. "Jason?"

"Don't use my name. They're listening. They always listen," he hissed, glancing around quickly.

"He threatened you?" Alex asked.

"Sorry, this is..." I started to introduce Alex, but he cut me short.

"I know who he is," Jason interrupted. "Remember, no names," he warned, continuing to speak. "He smiled while he did it, then the councilman started asking questions about my license and where I distribute my product. Real friendly-like."

"Why would he need to know that?" I asked.

"They were trying to squeeze out the campground. You shouldn't have reported the body," he said quietly.

"That's not something I could ignore, " I protested.

"I know," he said quickly. "That's why I called you. Not the cops. Not the paper. You don't pretend not to see things. You seek the truth."

"So why are you scared?" I asked.

Jason looked around the empty park, the tracks, the trees, and out into the rain.

"Because now they know you're paying attention," he said. "And people like Reed don't work alone."

A train whistle cut through the air, long and low.

"Just..." He hesitated. "Be careful who you trust. And if someone tells you to stop looking, ask yourself what they're afraid you'll find."

"Do you know if the fires are part of this?" I asked, still gripping Alex's hand tightly.

"Look into the kid." his eyes darted around again. "This conversation has been too long. I need to go." He turned and briskly walked away, taking the paved path out of sight.

Alex and I rushed back to the truck.

"That was weird," I said, once seat belted in for the short ride home.

"Looks like the town mooner pissed off Reed." Alex chuckled.

"Yeah, but he was really worried. That's not like him. I have a feeling Reed did more than just threaten him." I wrinkled my brow in thought.

"When we get home, I will check my email to see if the official report on the Martin fire has been finalized. Then we may need to make a stop by the shelter and talk to the kid like Jason suggested," Alex replied.

My phone flashed Kandice on the screen. I answered.

"How was the meeting?" she asked without saying hello.

"Good, Reed was a shady guy, like we suspected, but this whole thing could be bigger than just a bad-acting adjuster," I replied.

"Who was the mystery caller?"

"I will tell you when you stop by the house. He seemed to think we are all being watched."

"Okay, I just got out of class and I will head your way." She disconnected.

Robert was sitting in his Corvette when we pulled up to the condo. I waved as Alex parked the truck. We all piled out of the vehicles and tromped up the steps to my front door.

"Since I live here now, I really should have a key," Robert said as we filed into the entry and hung our coats.

I glanced at Alex. I wasn't sure how to proceed. Several months ago he stole my key and made himself at home whenever he wanted. We have made a lot of headway on what was allowed in our relationship and what was not, but a key to my house now too? I wasn't sure. The lack of an answer made him impatient.

"Well? I had to sit in the car for 30 minutes waiting for you two to show up."

"Only if you don't abuse your privileges with it this time," I warned, looking back at Alex, trying to see his reaction.

Alex's face had the usual unreadable expression. I suspect he was mentally throwing his hands in the air and giving up.

I handed Robert the key, but before letting it go, I hesitated.

"I won't behave like before. I promise. I really do care about you guys. Yes, I included you, Alex." Robert slyly grinned.

I let go of the key.

Alex placed his hand on Robert's shoulder. "Just remember, Taryn's the boss. What she says goes."

Robert shrugged Alex's hand off. "Some things have changed." He winked. "I remember things the other way around." He raised his eyebrows. "I'm willing to try new things." He grinned.

"Stop thinking those thoughts. I know what your dirty mind is doing," I pointed at him. It just made him grin wider. I rolled my eyes. "I assume your team was unsuccessful in finding the body?"

"Yep, we got as close to the fire zone as they would allow before we were kicked out of the area." He slipped off his muddy boots and placed them on the shoe tray.

I was struggling to balance and get my boots off. Alex had to hold my waist so I wouldn't fall over. Once I was stable, Alex went to the office to work on the Martin case. He needed to see what reports had come in. Investigating Brandon was becoming increasingly important.

"How was the mystery meeting?" Robert asked.

"It was Jason Moon," I replied.

"The mooner?"

"Yep, he was harassed by Reed Jackson and Councilman Thompson. He said 'they' are watching us and that corporations are trying to squeeze the campground out." I tried to recap the important stuff.

"Councilman Thompson has been leading the charge on the rezoning of areas in the city. I have had a few heated discussions at the city council meetings." Robert took a seat on the couch, patting the seat next to him and grinning.

I narrowed my eyes at him, but took a seat. "What zones are they changing?"

"Agricultural and residential in the valley to commercial, claiming 'economic growth' and 'for safety and development', " Robert air-quoted and grumbled. "Many of the residents don't even know this is happening. The council is quietly changing areas with the least population first, paving the way to take over the rest. Not all of the council agrees, but Thompson is all in and firmly believes this is the only way for Silver Springs to progress."

"It seems to me that Councilman Thompson would want to keep Reed around. He would have backed up the need for change. We should probably talk to him," I suggested.

A knock on the door, followed by Kandice entering, interrupted our conversation.

"Hey, what did I miss?"

Robert and I filled her in.

"The mooner is involved in this?" Kandice asked.

"I am not sure how involved, but the Thompsons have some explaining to do," I said.

Alex stepped out of the office, joining us in the living room. "The Fire Department sent over their report for the Martin's house. The origin does not appear consistent with lightning. If Jason says look into the kid, he must have known more than he told us."

"Do you really think some kid is lighting fires everywhere?" I asked.

"I don't know what to think just yet."

"Ryan mentioned going back tonight," Kandice said.

"He did. We could meet him and see what else he knows. I have several questions for him," I suggested.

Alex wrinkled his brow, "I don't think sneaking back out there is safe."

"How else are we going to talk to Ryan? No one knows where he is. He doesn't return phone calls, and he said he was going back." I pointed out.

"We won't go near the fire zone. We will stay in the base camp area," Kandice suggested. "Plus, I need to see if Trey is still there."

"I don't like it," Alex replied

"Honestly, I don't either," Robert added. "We spent the better part of the day out there today, and I don't think anywhere is safe."

"Then what do you suggest?" I asked, weirdly disappointed. I wasn't sure why either.

"Let me call David and see if there is any news," Alex suggested, pulling his phone out of his pocket and dialing David.

"Don't mention Jason. He didn't want the police to know." I pressed.

Alex gave me a disgruntled look. "Okay, for now," he said, waiting for David to pick up.

Robert headed for the kitchen. "Do you want anything to drink?" he asked.

"No, but thank you," I replied.

"Nope. I am good, too," Kandice said.

Kandice poked me. "We have to go back tonight," she whispered.

"I am not sure how we can manage that with these two." I gestured towards the boys.

Robert appeared next to me so quietly I didn't realize he was there until he brushed against me.

"It's nice to see you in my bed." He winked.

"This is my couch!" I pushed him, causing him to fall off. "Oh my gosh! Sorry, I didn't think I pushed you that hard." I reached out for him.

"Look's like you fell out of bed." Kandice giggled.

Robert stood up, straightened his shirt, and took his place beside me once more. "It was worth a shot," he grinned.

"Who do you know in the permitting office?" I asked mostly Robert, but the question was for both of them.

"Angie works there," Kandice replied.

"Angie Wilcox? I didn't realize she worked over there now. I thought she was still in real estate. She helped me get this place, remember?" Looks like we have an in. We need to go chat with her, see what she knows about the KOA and liquor license.

"She may not want to see me," Robert sheepishly added.

"You slept with her too?"

"Don't worry, it was after we broke up." He smiled.

I rolled my eyes. "The list never ends, does it?"

"Well, she's not any better." He pointed at Kandice.

"The difference is, I didn't pretend to be something that I wasn't," Kandice added.

"David hasn't been able to get into the restricted area yet. He has the judge looking at the attorney's request now," Alex announced.

"Well, Kandice and I need to go talk to Angie Wilcox. She works in the permits office. I want to see if I can get her to talk about what Councilman Thompson was trying to do to the campground and Jason's moonshine shop."

"It's already 4pm, they'll be closing soon. You should do that tomorrow," Alex suggested. "Catch her early so there's time to talk."

"Good point. Kandice, do you have class tomorrow?"

"Nope, just homework. I can get that done tonight." She smiled.

"If I remember correctly, she had a thing for sweets," I said, "Maybe we should stop at the bakery and pick up something for her."

"Oh, yeah, she did," Robert suggested, tracing her very curvy figure with his hands.

"How did that work out for you?" Kandice asked.

"It wasn't me who had the problem," Robert explained. "She's the one who thought one night wasn't good enough." He grinned.

"What are we talking about?" Alex asked, looking confused.

"Another one of Robert's victims," Kandice informed Alex.

"Hey, she was willing. I am not a bad guy," Robert protested.

"Got it." Alex was up to speed.

"Alex, let's run over to the shelter and see if we can talk to the Martins and Rosie. Then we can come back here, make dinner, and get ready for tomorrow. Kandice, you can do your homework, so you are free to hang with me tomorrow."

"What about me?" Robert asked.

"Get us a meeting with Councilman Thompson," I suggested.

"I will, but you will have to do what I say." His smile widened.

"Okay, whatever. Let's see what he knows."

Chapter 12

Alex and I left Kandice and Robert at my place and headed for the fairgrounds. We had evacuees to talk to. Once there, we check-in with Margery McNeal, the town's historic district president, the same Margery who Gramma was having over for tea tomorrow.

"Taryn, how are you? Your gramma keeps me up to date with all of your adventures." She smiled, her graying brown hair a teased ball of fluff sprayed into helmet perfection.

"Oh, you know Gramma, she sees everything as an adventure," I replied

"You must be Alex. I have heard a few things about you, too. You're her knight in shining armor." Margery chuckled.

"I am." He grinned.

"Are you here to serve with St. Bridget's Catholic Church?" she asked, looking at the check-in sheets, waiting to mark the correct one.

"No, I am here to see Rosie Sullivan and Ryan Newman," I answered.

Margery scanned the list, looking for the names. "Half the folks won't register. I am not seeing them on here."

"Weird, I talked to Rosie, and she said she was here. Can you check again?" I tried to read the list of names upside down on her clipboard.

Alex interjected, "I am actually here to see Brian Martin. I am working for him and need to speak with him."

Margery looked up from her clipboard, eyeing Alex. "Brian is on here. You may go." She motioned with her hand, allowing Alex to pass.

"The two you are looking for are not on the list," she said to me.

"She's still with me." Alex grabbed my arm, pulling me past Margery.

I could feel Margery's eyes on us as we wandered out of sight.

"She wasn't going to let me in. She is taking that gatekeeping job very seriously. I got the feeling she thought we were just listing names to get in," I ranted.

Alex listened to my complaining as he ushered me through the crowded evacuee camps inside the exhibition hall. Families, pet crates, cots, and sleeping bags were everywhere. I felt bad for these families. It was noisy and uncomfortable. My church group was set up in the concessions corner. Several ladies were in the little kitchen preparing dinner for the refugees.

We wove through the camps looking for the Martins, but my brain wasn't in the right place. All I could think about was why Rosie would lie about where she was.

Finally, we found them. Brian and his wife were playing cards, while Brandon, their son, was on his phone. He wore sweatpants and a hoodie that was pulled over his head. He was tucked against the wall. No one would even know he was there if they weren't looking for him. Brian saw us approaching and stood to greet us. Shaking our hands, he introduced us to his wife, Carolyn. Poking his son with his foot, he gestured for him to get up and meet us.

"The report came back as arson, just as we suspected," Alex said.

I stood quietly beside Alex and watched the seventeen-year-old's expression. His eyes darted around, but he stood in his sulky stature, not moving.

"Who would try to burn my place down?" Brian asked.

Carolyn was squeezing her hands together. Her nervous face appeared to be searching for answers.

"That's why I am here. There has been a tip, and I need permission to talk to Brandon."

Carolyn's eyes widened, and she threw her arms around the stiff teenager. "No way would Brandon have anything to do with this." She insisted.

"I agree with my wife. Brandon was in bed asleep when the fire broke out."

Brandon's face turned pale. He pulled at the collar of his hoodie.

"You need to find another lead. Whoever gave you that tip is lying," Brian said firmly, crossing his arms and shutting down the conversation.

"Sorry, I didn't mean to offend. We were not accusing Brandon of arson, we just wanted to see if he knew anything," Alex calmly replied.

"We will talk to our son. If anything of importance comes up, I will let you know," Brian replied.

"Thank you, Brian, Carolyn, Brandon." Alex nodded before turning and escorting me away from their little camp.

"That was weird," I said, once we were far enough away that they couldn't hear us.

"No, not really. Parents often have a hard time believing their child could be mixed up in anything bad, especially kids who are usually good," Alex replied. "If he is a good kid and had something to do with this, the pressure of the tip being called in will get him to crack."

"Was that your plan?" I asked, surprised Alex would be so calculating.

"Not initially. I had hoped he would just talk, but this is always the backup in these situations."

"Interesting." I grabbed his hand, and we headed for the exit. I really felt bad for these people. As we were leaving, I saw Jack in the coffee line.

"Jack, how's it going on the mountain?" I asked.

Jack moved forward in line, selecting a cardboard coffee cup. "Let me get my coffee, and then we will talk." He smiled. His blue eyes were calming.

Alex and I waited off to the side of the coffee station for Jack to fill his cup and add his creamer. Jack was in his fire uniform: navy cargo pants and Fire Station Four's polyester T-shirt, the words Fire and Rescue spread across his back. People kept approaching him, thanking him for everything the fire guys were doing to save our homes and community. He smiled his warm smile, his dimples deepened the wider the smile, as he shook everyone's hands.

"You being here brings comfort to them," I said as he approached, stirring his coffee with the little red stir stick. He tapped the stick twice before discarding it in the nearby trash bin.

"I hope so, but everyone wants answers, and we don't have any yet." He sighed.

"Nice to see you again, Jack. I never properly thanked you for patching her up." Alex motioned towards me.

"No worries, man, there is a lot going on these days. I haven't heard if they found the guy yet," Jack said.

"As of 1pm today, they had not," Alex replied.

"What's going on up there? The military moved in fast," I added, closing the gap in our little circle, hoping there weren't too many ears.

"We aren't being told. They brought in weather equipment, but that's not a huge surprise. Fires often create their own weather. It's all of the personnel and the restricted areas that are unnerving," Jack whispered. "Rumors are flying about what they are hiding and why they are here."

"What have you heard?" I asked, keeping my voice low.

"Just that someone was hired to start the fire so the lobbyist could push through the changes in insurance requirements. Others think investment firms are behind it. I don't really know what to think," he said.

"All the secrecy adds to the theories," Alex added.

"And the campground is at the center of it all," I whispered. "How's Scotty? I am worried about you all."

"He is fine. We haven't been on the front line since the federal wildland crews arrived. That's why I am here getting a break and breathing fresher air." He smiled, his radio came to life, "Engine two, report to ICP. Investigator requesting you."

"So much for the break and fresh air. Gotta run."

"Thanks, Jack." I could see my Aunt Suzy approaching us from the corner of my eye as I hugged Jack goodbye.

Aunt Suzy and my Uncle Patrick, my mom's brother, live a block over from my parents and almost always come over for Sunday dinner. Aunt Suzy volunteers for everything.

"Taryn, Alex." She waved. "A couple of the ladies from the church are running late. Could you come help in the kitchen?" she asked, her chestnut curls were pulled back into an unattractive hairnet, making her forehead look enormous. "You'll have to pull your hair back and wear one of these beauties, of course." She patted the ugly hairnet and grinned, her round face beaming with love.

I really didn't want to get stuck helping, and I frantically searched my brain for an excuse to get out of it, but as I looked around at the community on cots, how could I not? I looked at Alex. "If you can't stay because of work, come pick me up later," I said.

"I can make time to help out these poor people," he replied, turning to Aunt Suzy. "Plus, I have always wanted to sport one of those." He smirked.

That got Aunt Suzy to giggle before she handed me a hair tie, "Here, pull your hair back and follow me."

We wove through more family camps before arriving at the kitchen where Aunt Suzy announced, "I've got reinforcements!"

The Ladies Auxiliary of St. Bridget's Catholic Church were armed with hairnets, spoons, and casseroles galore.

I had to laugh. We looked ridiculous in our hairnets. The old women fawned over Alex, putting his muscles to work lifting, moving, and stacking casseroles into dietary categories. The leader of the pack, Theodora, was 85 years old and in heaven, directing the group. "We start serving in T-minus four minutes, everyone! Make sure your stations are ready," she announced.

The group cheered! I looked over at Alex. He appeared to be enjoying these funny old ladies. I smiled. Everyone took their spots, ready to serve over 100 meals. I was placed on potato casserole duty halfway down the line next to Mary Thatcher, who volunteered everywhere. I bet she's heard something about Ryan, the fires, or the adjuster.

"Mary, have you seen Ryan? I thought he would be here, but I haven't seen him," I asked, as the line of hungry, wayward citizens started to form.

"I haven't seen Ryan, but the KOA campground seems to be the center of this mess. I have friends who are on search and rescue, and they found explosives. Can you imagine?" Her hazel eyes widened beneath her thick glasses.

"No, that's terrible. Who would do such a thing?" I asked, acting surprised.

"Well," Mary started to say, but we were interrupted by our serving duties.

"Hello, would you like some cheesy potatoes?" I asked as the first person came through the line.

"Yes, please. Thank you so much for doing this." The woman smiled.

"Anything to make your situation a little better," I said.

The line seemed to go on forever. I tried to listen to the line gossip, but it was so noisy and everyone was uneasy. The only recurring theme was that this was going to drive up insurance rates and force everyone out. There was a darker undertone brewing. The missing adjuster, Reed Jackson, was on everyone's hit list. No one cared he was missing, and several said he got what he deserved. Reed had made enemies out of just about everyone in the valley.

I had been scooping potatoes for almost an hour. Alex had restocked my dish at least five times before our reinforcements arrived. They were hair-netting up, getting ready to relieve us. I turned to Mary, "You had something you were going to say about the fires earlier. What was it?" I asked as Alex swapped out my empty casserole dish again.

Mary leaned closer, lowering her voice even though the room was loud enough to drown out a confession.

"Oh yes. Well. My neighbor's sister works at City Hall." She glanced down the line before continuing. "Apparently, there was already a commercial expansion packet drafted for that corridor. Camp World's been circling for months."

I kept scooping potatoes. "Drafted?"

"Mm-hmm." She nodded knowingly. "All they needed was an emergency declaration to move it up on the agenda. Fires qualify."

My hand paused mid-scoop.

"They're calling it expedited review," she continued. "Safety, infrastructure reassessment, land viability. All very official sounding. But once they stamp it an emergency, public comment shortens. Votes happen faster."

I forced a smile at the next person in line. "Cheesy potatoes?" I asked, my mind racing with questions.

"Yes, please." A young girl stood smiling, holding her plate up.

Alex tapped my shoulder. "Time to put down your serving spoon."

Theodora was directing the relief volunteers all while keeping the line moving smoothly. I handed the spoon to my replacement. She thanked us again for helping. Peeling off the hairnet and gloves, I tossed them in the trash on our way out.

"That was crazy. I feel so bad for those people," I said.

"Wait!" I could see Aunt Suzy waving and trying to balance two smaller trays of food.

Alex went to her rescue, grabbing the trays from her.

"This is for you. We have plenty, and you helped us out." She smiled.

"Thank you." I hugged her.

Aunt Suzy skirted back to the kitchen area.

"This is nice. Now we have food for everyone at home." I smiled.

We piled into the truck, and I filled Alex in on my conversation with Mary on the drive home.

Chapter 13

I placed the trays of food on the bar while Kandice retrieved our plates and utensils.

"I got us a meeting with Councilman Thompson and his wife tomorrow night. Dinner reservations at The Sterling Elk at Alpine 85," Robert informed me as he grabbed napkins for everyone.

"How did you get us reservations there? Everyone knows the waitlist is months long." My eyes widened with excitement. The Sterling Elk is the fanciest restaurant in Silver Springs. It's part of the Alpine 85 ski resort. I usually only get to go there if a party I'm planning wants them. They are also very expensive.

Robert smirked. "It's me, do you really have to ask that?"

Kandice rolled her eyes. "There you go, you're letting his ego grow."

Alex eyed Robert. "Why that restaurant?"

"Because it was fancy enough to dangle in front of the pompous councilmen. I figured he would have a hard time turning it down." Robert smiled.

"That, plus you knew it would just be you and Taryn." Alex looked annoyed.

"Maybe?" Robert shrugged.

Alex's phone rang. It was David.

"Saved by the bell." Kandice giggled, filling up her plate with chicken and rice casserole and taking a seat at the table. I followed her.

"Okay, does that mean we found something?" Alex asked.

We all strained to hear, but Alex wasn't saying much, just nodding in agreement. He hung up and turned to me, rubbing the back of his neck. "The judge lifted the temporary block on the KOA perimeter. Search and Rescue is being called back in." He turned to Robert, "Looks like we're needed out there again." Directing his attention back to me, he asked, "You going to be okay here?"

"Yep, we will be just fine. It's you two I am worried about." I knew this would give me the opportunity to try to meet with Ryan, but I still didn't like them being out there.

"I will call you as soon as I know something," Alex replied.

The boys quickly took a couple of bites of food and changed. Alex kissed me, and they were gone only minutes after David's call. Kandice and I finished dinner and picked up the kitchen before she ran home to change. I called Ryan, leaving a message, letting him know I would be at the parking lot at 10pm.

Kandice picked me up. I dressed in black this time. I wasn't sure what I was going to do when, or if, I saw Ryan. We parked in the parking lot again and waited until we saw him. He appeared from the woods and was covered in dirt. He didn't wave. He just motioned for us to join him at the edge of the forest.

Stepping out of the Jeep, I rapid-fired questions at him. "Where have you been? You never returned my calls? Are you okay?"

"Keep your voice down. I had to stay hidden. I don't want to involve you any further, so I am here to say, stay out of this. You don't want to end up like Reed," Ryan replied harshly.

"Are you threatening us?" Kandice accused.

I grabbed her hand. She was tense with rage. "Just tell us what's going on."

"I got a Notice of Land Use Review the same day the fire started." He wiped dirt from his face.

"What kind of review?" I asked.

"Land compatibility assessment." He gave a short, humorless laugh. "They're deciding whether I still belong here."

"They can't just change it," I said. "You've been here forever."

"I'm grandfathered in," he said quickly. "This campground was here before most of those houses."

"Then you're protected," Kandice said.

"Protected?" His eyes flicked towards the orange glow of the mountainside. "They've flagged this area for commercial expansion. Camp World's been pushing for it for months. This fire just made it easier."

The smoke was thick and hung in the air.

"If they can argue the fire made the land unsafe, or claim there's substantial damage, they can fast-track the review," he continued, his voice a low growl. "Once everything around me goes commercial, I become the nonconforming use."

"And if there's substantial damage?" I prompted.

"They don't have to let me rebuild the way it was." His gaze settled on me, but it was unreadable. "They can make it so I can't rebuild at all," he growled. "Do you understand what that means, Taryn?" It wasn't just frustration in his voice. It was anger. His jaw flexed. "It's survival."

Silence settled between us, thick as the smoke drifting through the trees.

For the first time, I couldn't tell if Ryan was just a man being cornered... or a man who had already decided how far he was willing to go.

"I want you to leave," he said, turning and disappearing into the night.

We stood in silence, listening to the wind.

"Do you think he killed Reed?" Kandice finally asked.

"My initial feeling was no, but now I am not so sure," I said reluctantly.

"He wasn't with us when we found the body." Kandice pointed out.

"That's part of my concern." I rubbed my hands across my arms, trying to warm myself. "I am afraid we have just reached the tip of the iceberg with this whole thing." A shiver ran down my spine.

I wasn't sure what to do next. Kandice and I lingered in the parking lot a while longer.

"Should we go find Trey?" Kandice finally asked.

I hesitated. I wasn't sure that was a good idea. We would be crossing into the fire evacuation zone, and this time it didn't feel so safe. But telling Kandice not to look for her boyfriend felt worse. I certainly wouldn't stop if it were Alex.

Reluctantly, we headed down the same trail we'd taken the last night with Ryan. The machinery noise was just as before, engines idling and generators humming. It felt too easy to slip into the military camp unnoticed. If the government were involved, surely they had this place secured. We hung back in the trees, blending in as best we could in our black clothing, hoping to stay unnoticed.

A large, shadowed figure stepped out from behind one of the trailers and dropped into a folding chair outside. He leaned forward, elbows on his knees, face buried in his hands.

"I think that's Trey," Kandice whispered.

We crept closer.

"Trey?" she called softly.

He didn't move at first.

"Trey." She tried again, louder this time.

The figure stood abruptly and walked towards us.

"Kandice? Is that you?"

Relief flooded her voice. "Yes."

He stopped just before the trees.

"Why did you lie to me?" she asked, her voice already shaking.

"I didn't have a choice," Trey replied quietly. "It's my job. I have a classification level for restricted access. They don't give you that kind of access if you blab. They know they can trust me, and you being here compromises that trust."

"But you lied to me."

"Not because I wanted to."

She looked like she might cry, which was rare for Kandice.

"I was worried. I've never felt this way about someone before. I don't know if I can handle this... this secrecy, even if it is for work. It never bothered me until now. You're home. In my home." Kandice's voice was about to crack.

"I don't know what to say. This has been our relationship. I can't change that," He answered softly.

"Then just tell me you're on a government job here in Silver Springs. Stay with me. You don't have to explain details."

"I can't," he said. "I'm staying here. I'm camped in one of these trailers because this situation is bigger than you realize. They're watching everything. They probably already know I'm talking to you. I need you to go," he continued. "And I need you to trust me."

"Are you ever going to be able to tell me what you actually do?" she asked.

"Most of what I do, I can never speak about."

"So this is our life? I just trust you forever? Not knowing where you are? Not knowing if you're okay?" Her voice cracked. "When you said you worked for the government, I pictured a government facility somewhere and computer work. I had no idea you were traveling around, living out of campers in the middle of wildfires."

"Please," he said, "we can't do this right now."

I gently tugged Kandice's arm. "He's right. Not tonight."

She resisted for a second, then exhaled.

Trey pulled her close and kissed her, as if he wasn't sure he'd get another chance. "We'll talk when this is over. I'll tell you everything I'm allowed to. I'm not promising it'll be much. But what I can say will be the truth."

He stepped back towards the trailers. Kandice didn't move. I wrapped my arms around her, holding my friend for a moment. I didn't know how she was going to handle this. Kandice was promiscuous in the past, leading only with her head. She had always controlled her relationships. If things went sideways, she walked away first, protecting herself from heartbreak. This was different. She could not control this. This time her heart was in charge.

We walked back to the Jeep in silence.

"Can I say one thing?" I asked as I climbed into the Jeep. "He very clearly loves you."

"I know," she sighed, starting the engine, "It's just... it was easier when I thought he was in a building, nerding out, not actually off the grid."

"Remember, Scarlet O'Hara, don't think about it today, think about it tomorrow. Once this whole thing is behind us, you'll know what to do." I smiled.

"Maybe you're right."

"Of course I am right. When have I ever not been right?

She eyed me, smirking.

"Okay, don't answer that." I grinned. "I am right about this."

She nodded. "I'll pick you up in the morning. We're still going to talk to Angie, correct?"

"Yep, I want to see this expansion packet for myself."

The headlights cut through the darkness as we drove back towards town. My thoughts swirled with all the scandals surrounding this. The fire wasn't the only thing spreading.

My phone rang just as Kandice pulled away from my house. It was Alex. I dropped onto the couch and took the call.

"We found him." Alex coughed.

"Dead?" I was pretty sure I knew the answer.

"Unfortunately, yes," Alex replied.

"Where was he?" I asked

"There's a deep ravine on the other side of the ridge, behind the campground." Alex coughed again. "The smoke is getting thick out here. We have recovered him, and Search and Rescue has been sent home. I am staying a bit longer to help David. Robert should be home soon."

"Okay, do we know if it was foul play?" I asked, twirling a piece of my hair between my fingers.

"It's highly suspicious. We suspect the coroner will confirm our suspicions. He should be here in a few minutes."

"I talked to Ryan briefly. He said he got a Notice of Land Use Review the same day the fire started. That fits Mary's expansion packet knowledge." I said, leaning back onto the couch.

"Where is Ryan?" Alex asked.

"He said to stay out of this. He doesn't want me to end up like Reed. I don't know where he is," I replied, I knew Alex would not like that.

There was silence for a moment.

"Taryn, lock the doors, let Robert use his key to get in, and do not leave, please. I don't like the sound of any of this," Alex pleaded with me.

"I have all of the doors locked. I am not leaving, and I will be fine. You just be safe and come home as soon as possible."

"I love you," he said.

"I love you, too," I replied.

I let out a sigh. Giselle meowed at my feet and hopped up on the couch, snuggling in next to me. She purred. "All of this seems off," I said to my cat, giving her a gentle scruff on her fluffy cheek. She closed her eyes without giving me any answers or ideas of what to do next. "A lot of help you are." I laughed.

The doorknob jiggled as Robert let himself in.

"Honey, I'm home," he sang out.

I rolled my eyes and smiled.

"That was a real treat. We could have done that during the daylight if that attorney hadn't blocked everything," Robert complained.

"Was he found in the blocked zone?" I asked.

Robert stood in the foyer, removing his dirty boots and coat. "Nope, just past it. But the best access was through the blocked zone."

"Do you think it really was murder?"

"Probably. It makes the most sense. He certainly didn't die from the fall into the ravine. I am going to jump in the shower," he said as he headed towards the bathroom.

I yawned, standing up and stretching. I knocked on the bathroom door.

"You never have to knock," Robert hollered.

I ignored him. "I am going to bed. I will see you in the morning," I said through the door.

"Good night."

Chapter 14

Alex had arrived home early in the morning, and I had no idea how late it was. He was still sleeping when I got up to get ready for my meeting with Angie Wilcox. Kandice picked me up, and we headed to the Belgian Bakery on Second Street. They had the best pastries in town. The moment we stepped inside the little shop, the warm scent of butter and sugar filled our nostrils, the pastry-laden air making our mouths water before we even spotted the pastry case. After selecting an assortment of goodies, we opted to order coffee and eat our food in the corner booth, where we could privately chat about how we were going to get Angie to talk. After what felt like a breakfast so good it should have been illegal, we headed to the permitting office.

City Hall was on the south side of town. It had been relocated to its current building about ten years ago when they felt they had outgrown the old historic building in the center of town.

The original building was made into a museum holding all of Silver Springs' history.

The new city hall was modern and sterile compared to the previous stone and brick building. We entered the glass doors and followed the signs to the permitting department. It was on the second floor in the west wing. Taking the west side elevators, we approached the office door with etched black letters spelling Permitting. I could see Angie at the desk through the glass door.

"Good morning," I said as I walked through the door, Kandice following close behind me.

Angie's plump, round face smiled. "Taryn, Kandice, it's been a while."

"It has," Kandice replied.

"We had breakfast at the Belgian Bakery before stopping by here and thought you might like some pastries." I smiled, holding up the box filled with fat, sugar, and joy.

"That is so sweet of you guys. You remembered I do love a good pastry." She reached for the box. "What brings you by this morning?" she asked.

"Well, I have been working on the KOA reopening picnic and barbecue, but with this fire, everything is postponed until next weekend, that is, if they get this fire under control."

"I just saw the news announced no new growth overnight, and it's twenty-five percent contained now." Angie interrupted.

"That's fantastic news!" I had not heard that yet.

"I also heard that Reed Jackson was found dead," she said, eyeing the pastry box.

"The news didn't say it was Reed this morning," Kandice replied.

"I know, I am reading between the lines. Reed was missing, and now a body was recovered. One can only assume," she said, selecting the chocolate-filled croissant.

"Since we're on the subject of Reed, rumor has it he pushed for a land reassessment and filed an expansion packet for the valley," I prompted.

Her eyes darted around, and she leaned closer, motioning for us to join her. "He met with Councilman Thompson several times regarding properties Neighborhood Integrity had flagged as 'high risk'," she whispered, taking a bite of the croissant. "These are delicious. Would you like to share?" She held the box up.

"No, we ate earlier. How fast does this all happen?" Kandice asked.

"The city's been lining up a full land reassessment, safety, fire, and infrastructure over the last few months. Normally it'd drag on, but the fire emergency lets them push it through fast."

"What do you mean?" I whispered, still leaning over the counter slightly.

"Outside counsel submitted an expansion packet," Angie continued. "They're using the fire to fast-track the review, so everything's moving sooner than normal."

"Without council approval?" Kandice asked.

"No," Angie shrugged. "They still need to vote and notify residents, but the emergency rules make it easier to move approvals along quickly."

"Can you tell me who the outside counsel is?" I asked, hoping she could.

"I can do better." She smiled slyly. "I can give you a copy of the packet for a $10 service fee. It's public record."

Angie typed away on her computer. Moments later, the printer behind her buzzed to life. She stood retrieving the papers, stapling and stamping them. "That will be $10. If you are using a card, there will be a 3.5% service fee incurred." She held her hand out.

I pulled out my credit card. I was, unfortunately, out of cash. Angie swiped the card, printed the receipt, and handed the packet over to me.

"Hey, Taryn, why do you want to know this stuff? Your family lives over on Third," she questioned.

"Let's just say I am doing it for a friend," I said.

She eyed Kandice and me. "Sure, sure. It's not like you two haven't been involved in espionage before." She smirked.

My face flushed. "It's not like that," I lied, a little too defensively.

Kandice came to my rescue, grabbing my hand. "Thanks, Angie, we gotta go. Enjoy the pastries," she said over her shoulder while dragging me out the door.

"I can't believe Angie was so willing to let us have this," I said as we climbed into the Jeep.

"And I can't believe public records cost ten dollars plus a three-and-a-half percent fee just to be allowed to have them," Kandice replied. "That's ridiculous."

"I thought we'd have to convince her to even talk to us."

Once we were settled into our seats, we flipped through the packet. The letterhead immediately caught my attention.

"Salgner and Kats," I said, tapping the top of the page. "That's the same name Rosie mentioned. She said this firm was harassing Ryan."

"You didn't tell me Ryan was being harassed by an attorney," Kandice said.

"I guess I forgot. Rosie told me yesterday on the phone."

"Was that before or after you discovered she wasn't at the fairgrounds?"

"Before. And just because Margery didn't see her name on the list doesn't mean she wasn't there," I replied, still scanning over the document.

"Did you see her there?" Kandice asked.

"Well, no," I admitted. "But I was a little busy."

Kandice gave me a look. "How did Rosie end up working for Ryan?"

"I'm not sure. I haven't worked with Ryan in years. The campground's always been a good seasonal job for high school and college kids. It makes sense she'd work there. It's temporary.

Most of them leave once school starts. One year, he even hired an older couple who wanted to stay the whole season and run the front desk. I can't remember their names."

I flipped another page. "This expansion packet looks like they're trying to convert the entire valley to commercial use. I know Camp World wanted to buy the KOA from Ryan. They've been pressuring him for months."

"Do you think this is the same attorney's office that blocked the Search and Rescue?" Kandice asked.

"It would make sense. But it says 'client property.' Who's the client? Maybe Ryan hired them." As I said it, something felt off.

"Maybe Rosie got it wrong." Kandice shrugged. "Maybe he wasn't being harassed. Maybe he retained them."

"That could explain the language. But this isn't just about Ryan's property." I scanned the pages. "The land assessment request and expansion packet goes into detail about fire dangers, rising insurance rates, and surrounding properties not meeting safety standards. There are a lot of accusations here. This covers the entire valley."

"Last night, Trey said this is bigger than we thought, but he couldn't tell us what's going on. Do you think he knows?" Kandice asked.

"It doesn't make sense for the military to move in that quickly without a reason. And remember Ryan saying he heard people arguing and saying 'he'd made a big mess of things and they'd have to spin it in their favor'?"

"Oh, I remember," Kandice said. "But I also remember a man was found dead on his property, and Ryan had blood on him."

"I know, and I'm not ruling that out. I'm just trying to piece everything together and see if something clicks." I stared out the window. "Jason said to look into the kid. And the Martins got awfully defensive when we questioned him."

"So is that just good parenting," Kandice questioned, "or are they hiding something?"

She pulled over her seatbelt, clicking it in place. I did the same.

"Exactly. My mom and gramma are having tea with Margery today to discuss the new fire code proposal requiring gramma to remove her rose bushes. Maybe we should stop by afterward and see what they've heard."

"That's a great idea. I haven't seen your mom in weeks, and I love your gramma," Kandice chirped. "She'll know what's going on."

"Let's head home and let the boys look at this expansion packet. We need to decide what to do next. Plus, I need to get some actual work done. All this running around is throwing off my schedule."

Kandice smirked. "You and your color-coded calendar. Fourteen checklists, double-checklists, triple-checklists. You're fine."

I smiled. She knew me too well. "I still need to catch up. And I don't know if Alex has uncovered anything new on the Martin's case. It would be good to compare that with this expansion packet."

"I agree. Let's go." Kandice put the Jeep in gear, taking South Main to head home.

The rain had finally stopped, and patches of blue sky were breaking through the clouds. It had only been a few days of steady rain, but for Colorado, that felt like an eternity.

When I opened my front door, I found Alex and Robert seated at my table with Detective David Parker, papers spread out everywhere.

"What are you boys working on?" I asked, slipping off my coat as Kandice followed behind me. "Looks like some serious investigating."

Detective Parker glanced up, looking tired and unamused, but focused. He didn't comment.

I pulled up a barstool between Alex and Robert, while Kandice took the empty chair. The five of us gathered around the table.

"What are we looking at?" I asked.

"Plot maps," Robert said. "Where the body was first found and where it was ultimately discovered. We're trying to determine why it was moved, how quickly it could've been moved, and how far from the original location."

"The wind's supposed to shift today," Detective Parker added. "If that happens, the fire could move back towards town. I'll be heading out shortly to check for additional evidence. I wanted this mapped out first."

"Are you going with him?" I asked Alex.

"Probably. What's that you've got?" Alex asked, nodding towards the papers in my hand.

I placed the packet in the center of the table. "This is the expansion packet and land assessment filed the day of the fire."

"What?" Robert said.

"My thoughts exactly. We'd heard rumors about a land grab in the valley, so Kandice and I talked to Angie in permitting. The rumors appear to be true," I said, bringing Detective Parker up to speed on my shenanigans, as he liked to call it.

David picked up the packet and flipped through it before handing it to Alex.

"Is this the same attorney who blocked your search and rescue?" I asked.

David rubbed his temples and sighed. "Yes. Same firm. They temporarily halted our operation."

"I knew it," Kandice said.

Robert leaned over the pages. "They're citing multiple properties for fire risk violations and pushing to bring them up to code. The KOA appears to be under a special permit. It's not zoned the same as the others."

"That's probably because it was established before much of the valley," David said. "Likely grandfathered in."

"That explains the reassessment," I said.

"And it gives Ryan motive." David pointed out.

"But someone's been setting these fires. You found small ignition points. Could Ryan really be behind that, too?" I asked.

"I'm not ready to draw conclusions," David said. "I'm still gathering evidence. But something out there isn't right."

"Ever since Reed moved here and started re-assessing homes and denying claims," Robert added, "he's been attending council meetings and pushing for rezoning under the banner of fire mitigation. Mitigation is one thing. Full commercial rezoning? That's another. It doesn't line up with his role as an insurance adjuster."

"Where exactly was Reed found?" I asked, pointing to the map.

"About one hundred yards from where you were when you discovered him," David said.

"Someone had moved him that far?" Kandice asked. "Unless he wasn't dead and managed to stumble."

"That's what the coroner is trying to determine," David replied.

Chapter 15

Kandice may have made fun of me and all my color-coded checklist glory, but I really did have a lot of work to do. I had four weddings scheduled in June, one of them only five weeks away. There were so many details to finish up to make sure they were exactly right. Phone calls to make. Emails to send.

My mother wouldn't be hosting tea with Margery until about two, which meant I had the better part of the day to work.

Robert had disappeared on some errands. He said he had to run out for a while. I didn't really ask what he was doing. I was too busy to care. Not in a mean way. I was working when he popped his head in the office and said he was leaving and had things to do.

Kandice needed to stop by the advisor's office and work out her summer enrollment schedule. Going back to school at twenty-six, working part-time, and trying to keep up with the Charlie's Angel image of us was keeping her busy. Honestly, I am surprised I have seen her so much.

I was halfway through answering emails when Alex stuck his head into the office.

"Are you busy?" he asked, smiling.

"Why?" I said, eyeing him suspiciously.

He leaned against the doorway with a smirk. "The last couple of days have been a little crazy. We actually have the house to ourselves. I thought maybe..." He raised an eyebrow.

I shook my head, trying not to laugh. Standing from my chair, I skipped over to him, throwing my arms around his neck. He ran his hands down my waist, kissing my collarbone, making me turn to jello in his arms. He scooped me up and carried me to the bedroom.

We lay in a twisted mess under the covers.

"Can I ask you a question?" I said, still wrapped in his arms.

"Of course." He released me so I could turn around and face him.

"What do you think is going on around here?"

"I think whoever set the fires is our killer."

"Unless Reed was told to set the fires and someone killed him afterward so he couldn't talk, protecting their interests." I gazed into his honey-colored eyes. There was something so comforting in them. I always felt so safe.

"I'm a little nervous about dinner tonight with Councilman Thompson," I admitted. "He seems to be the only one who might know exactly what's happening. I'm not saying he killed Reed.

It doesn't make sense that he would, but he's involved in all the city permitting and paperwork. He has to know something."

Alex studied me for a second.

"Why are you worried?" he said with a small grin. "I'd like to see his reaction when you start asking the questions I know you're going to ask."

"I don't know. It's just unsettling for some reason. I wish you were coming with me."

"I wish I were coming too."

"Robert set it up this way." I rolled my eyes. "He thinks it will look less suspicious. Did you know he actually told me he's my bodyguard now?"

Alex laughed. "He's persistent, if nothing else. You know, you could tell him you don't want to go. Or that you want me to come with you."

I shrugged. "I don't know. Maybe Robert's right, maybe it's better this way. Councilman Thompson is used to seeing him at the city council meetings. I had no idea Robert went to those."

"It makes sense for him to go to dinner with you," Alex replied, kissing my forehead. "You'll do great, and honestly, I know he will keep you safe if anything goes wrong."

I nodded slowly. "It'll be... sneaky."

I stretched. "I have to finish my emails, then we should pay Jason a visit. I have a few questions for him. Mostly about how he knew Reed and why he told us to look into the kid, Brandon.

"I like that plan," Alex replied. "And I need to circle back over to the fairgrounds too. See if Brandon is feeling like talking yet. The news is out that the adjuster is dead. Maybe that'll put a little pressure on him."

"The news hasn't mentioned arson yet," I said.

"No. I doubt it will for a while."

"Unless I leave a tip," I said with a sly smile.

Alex laughed. "That could stir up some things."

"Racheal at the newspaper was really hoping I'd give her something," I said.

"What would you even say? We don't know what we're dealing with yet."

"I don't know. Just that I have it on good authority arson is highly suspected for the fires in the valley." I wrinkled my nose. "And hope she is willing to post it."

Jason's shop wasn't all that far from my house, so we decided to walk. The blue sky had finally pushed back the clouds, and the sun felt good on our backs. It was a bit of a stroll, but not long enough to bother driving. Besides, I needed some fresh air. Silver Springs still smelled faintly of smoke, but it reminded me more of campfires and s'mores than danger. Alex and I walked hand in hand down the street, turned onto Main, and continued several blocks until we reached Jason's moonshine shop.

The place sat in the alley between Second Avenue and Main Street. The front of the shop looked like a normal souvenir store full of Silver Springs memorabilia. But the real attraction was hidden in the back. To get there, you had to walk through a door marked Employees Only that looked like a storage closet. Once inside, the room opened into a full speakeasy-style moonshine bar.

Jason had decorated the place like something straight out of the 1920s. Shelves were stacked with mason jars of moonshine, each with fun names tied to Silver Springs. My personal favorite was the strawberry rhubarb pie shine. It tasted exactly like strawberry rhubarb pie and was inspired by the rhubarb festival and pie contest the town of Ironcrest held every year.

When we entered the shop, Jason's eyes widened when he saw us. He started to turn around. Alex was faster and grabbed him by the arm. "Where do you think you're going? We have a few questions."

"Let go of me!" Jason snapped. "I told you what I know. I told you to be careful with what you're researching. These people are dangerous. Look what they did to Reed. I didn't even like the guy, but he's dead."

"How do we know you didn't do it?" Alex asked calmly, releasing his grip.

Jason stared at him. "Why would you suspect me?"

"You seemed to know Reed is dead," Alex said. "You knew Taryn found him. You said her brother told you, but you also know he's a firefighter, so you could have used that to your advantage. And you told us to look into the kid. So spill it. What else aren't you telling us?"

Jason looked over at me. "Is he serious?"

I shrugged. "He makes a good point. Why don't you tell us what you do know?"

Jason's eyes darted between Alex and me. He was thinking. Trying to decide how much he wanted to say.

"Look, Jason," I said. "I'm having dinner with Councilman Thompson tonight. If you're not involved in this, give me something. Anything that helps us understand what's going on. I already know about the commercial zoning efforts," I continued. "I know an expansion packet was filed. I know they're trying to force Ryan out of the KOA. What I don't understand is why Reed and Councilman Thompson were harassing you."

"You called Taryn. You are involved now whether or not you want to be," Alex said firmly.

Jason frowned. "I wish I hadn't now. It was thrilling at first, but now it's just stressful. I don't know why he started bothering me. I don't live in the valley and I don't have anything to do with permitting or zoning."

"What did he say?" I pressed.

"He said the Moon Map of Silver Springs was annoying and juvenile. He said a resort-style town didn't need that kind of publicity." Jason grabbed a T-shirt from a nearby rack and held it up. The shirt read I'VE BEEN MOONED BY THE MOONSHINER with two mason jars placed strategically.

"I just got these in a week ago," Jason said. "People love them. I sign them all the time. My butt's more famous than my moonshine."

I burst out laughing.

Alex even cracked a small smile.

"It's ridiculous," I said.

Jason shrugged. "For whatever reason, Reed had it out for me. He wanted my shop closed. Wanted my liquor license pulled."

"I still don't understand. Why?" I asked.

Jason thought about it. "The only thing I can think of," he said slowly, "is that I sell my moonshine at the little liquor store at the KOA campground." He shrugged again. "Maybe he didn't want alcohol being sold out there."

"That doesn't explain the threats," Alex said.

Jason nodded. "I know. He said if the campground closed, the liquor license out there might not survive the transition anyway."

"The transition to what?" I asked.

Jason shook his head. "Your guess is as good as mine. All I know is Reed acted like something big was coming to Silver Springs. Something he thought would make this place a lot fancier than it is now."

"I am still fuzzy on why you. You are not the only liquor store in town." I pointed out.

"Look around," he said, gesturing to the jars of moonshine lining the shelves. "I run a speakeasy with a moonshine theme and sell T-shirts with my backside on them. Reed already thought I was ruining the town's reputation."

Alex crossed his arms. "Tell us about the kid."

"What do you want to know?" Jason sighed.

"Why did you tell us to look into him?"

"Brandon and a couple of his friends came into the shop. They were browsing the souvenirs when Reed showed up. Reed pulled Brandon aside and talked to him privately. I couldn't hear what they said."

"Then what happened?" I asked.

"They shook hands."

"They shook hands," I repeated. "And?"

"And what? It looked like they made some kind of deal," Jason said.

"That's why you told us to look into the kid?" I asked.

Jason shrugged. "Well, yeah. Why else would Reed pull him aside like that?"

"Could've been anything," Alex said. "Maybe he knew him."

"Maybe," Jason said. "Or maybe not."

Jason leaned back against the counter. "Look, maybe I overreacted. Maybe there's nothing there."

"You expect me to believe that?" I asked, growing more annoyed. Something about this didn't sit right with me.

Alex stayed quiet, arms still crossed.

"Look," Jason remained leaning against the counter, "I told you what I did because I know something is, or was, I guess, up with Reed. Everyone seems to like my brand except him and the councilman."

"Listen, Jason, if you hear or see anything else, let me know. Maybe look into your license since that seems to be your connection with them," I said before turning to exit the shop.

He gave a short nod, but I could tell he wasn't thrilled with the situation. None of us were.

We stepped out of the shop. The sun was shining, but only a few people moved along the sidewalks. The usual small-town chatter felt muted. Everyone seemed to be watching the hills or checking their phones for updates about the fire.

"Let's hit the river trail and walk it over to the fairgrounds," I said as we strolled down Main Street. The river trail was on the east side of Main and it would take us along the water straight to the back of the shelter.

"Sounds like a plan to me," Alex agreed. "Hopefully, the Martins will be ready to chat.

I could see my brother, Scotty, when we got there. He was talking to the check-in guy. Margery wasn't hosting the check-in station this time because she was probably being interrogated by my gramma right now. I laughed at that. We really are more alike than I ever thought. We approached the table, and I picked up the pace. I hadn't seen my brother much over the last few days, and I was so happy to see him safe. I ran around the table and gave him a tight hug.

"I am so glad to see you are alright!" Then, I smacked his arm, "Why did you tell Mom I found Reed's body?" I glared at him. He was safe, now I could be mad at him.

"What? She asked. I didn't say anything else," he promised, shoving me in return.

Directing his attention to Alex and trying to ignore me, he greeted Alex with a handshake.

"This conversation is not over." I pointed at him and smiled.

"Alex, good to see you again. I'm glad to see my sister hasn't driven you crazy yet."

"Hey!"

"I don't scare that easily." Alex smiled. "We are here to see the Martins."

"I can see you are still investigating then, too." Scotty smirked, looking at me.

"So what can you tell me then?" I eyed Scotty.

"The winds are shifting back towards town. We have set up a burn line trying to protect the homes. Our federal and military friends are monitoring the situation and are as positive as you can be with fire." Scotty smiled.

"What about the arson?" I asked.

"The fire inspector is going over the evidence. It's a slow process, especially since the fire isn't out yet," he explained.

I frowned and wrinkled my nose in thought.

"Patience was never your virtue." He cracked a grin.

I narrowed my eyes at him. "Not funny."

Alex stood quietly, not interrupting our banter.

"I actually have to head back out there. I was here for a short breather," he said.

"Be safe." I hugged him once more.

Alex and I found the Martins sitting at one of the long folding tables inside the fairground's exhibition hall. The evacuation shelter buzzed with quiet conversations, the hum of portable fans, and the occasional clatter of someone setting down a tray from the volunteer food line.

Brandon sat slouched in a metal chair, staring at the floor. His parents sat across from him, their faces tired and drawn from too many sleepless nights.

Brian Martin noticed us first. His shoulders stiffened.

"We already told you," he said before we even reached the table. "Our son didn't see anything."

He was obviously still disgruntled about yesterday's conversation.

"I remember," Alex said evenly. "And I'm not here to accuse Brandon of anything." Pulling out a chair, he motioned for me to sit. He sat in the chair across from Brian.

Carolyn Martin looked between us. "Then what do you want?" she questioned.

Alex pulled out his phone, swiping through photos, he handed the phone to Brian.

"What is this?" Brian frowned. Carolyn leaned over to take a look.

"It's part of an expansion packet filed with the city. Commercial zoning proposals, land re-assessments, safety reviews for the entire valley," Alex explained.

Brian skimmed the page, his expression darkening. "What does this have to do with us?"

Alex leaned back slightly in his chair. "It means someone's been putting pressure on property owners, threatening inspections, rezoning, insurance problems, and Reed Jackson seems to have been in the middle of a lot of those conversations," Alex continued calmly.

Brandon shifted in his seat. Carolyn's eyes flicked towards her son.

I noticed it. Alex noticed it too.

"We spoke with Jason Moon earlier," he said. "The owner of the moonshine shop."

Brian scoffed. "What's that got to do with anything?"

"He told us Reed had been threatening him," Alex said. "Trying to shut down his shop. Pull his liquor license."

"So, Reed was making enemies all over town," Brian muttered.

"Possibly," Alex said, letting the silence sit for a moment before continuing. "But what interests me is that Reed also told people their properties might not pass inspection if they didn't cooperate," Alex said. He was speculating, but the Martins didn't need to know that.

Brandon's head dropped a little lower.

"Brandon," Alex said quietly, "did Reed ever speak to you alone?"

The boy didn't answer.

Brian turned towards him. "Brandon?"

Carolyn started to interrupt, but Brian stopped her. "We hired him to find out the truth, even if we don't like it. Brandon what are you not telling us?" Brian questioned his son.

The boy's foot started tapping nervously under the table.

"Brandon," Alex said, "did Reed tell you your property might fail an inspection?"

The boy swallowed. "Yes."

The word came out barely above a whisper.

Carolyn looked at him in shock. "What?" she asked.

Brandon rubbed his hands together. "He told me the valley was going to change. He said that developers were coming. He said our house might not pass the next review." Brandon sat up straight. "I knew how stressed out you guys were about this insurance stuff."

Carolyn's face paled. "And then?"

"He showed me pictures." Brandon hesitated.

Brian frowned. "Pictures of what?"

"From a party." he muttered. "Me and some friends. Drinking." Brandon looked miserable.

Brian's face turned red.

"He said he'd report it." Brandon rushed on. "He said I'd get charged for underage drinking and it would follow me."

"And what did he ask you to do?" Alex prompted.

"He gave me this igniter thing," he said quietly.

Carolyn gasped, "Brandon, what did you do?"

"He said to start a small fire in the trees behind our house," Brandon continued, his voice was shaking now. "Just a little one."

Brian stared at him in disbelief.

"He promised it wouldn't reach the house," Brandon said quickly. "He said firefighters were already nearby."

The table went silent.

"You started the fire?" Brian asked hoarsely.

"He said it would only burn one tree." Brandon tried to defend himself. "He said we would be protected if I did this."

I felt my stomach twist. The poor kid was manipulated and blackmailed.

"Thank you for telling us the truth." Brian placed his hand on his son's shoulder.

Brandon looked like he might collapse. "I didn't think it would spread like that," he whispered.

For the first time since we'd walked into the shelter, the Martins weren't angry anymore. They were scared. And suddenly the fires in the valley made a lot more sense. If Reed had convinced Brandon to set a fire, how many others did he convince?

Chapter 16

K andice picked me up from the fairgrounds. Alex wasn't done yet. He still had paperwork to finish and a few loose ends to tie up for the Martins. Brandon's confession answered the biggest question, but it didn't make the situation any easier for the family. He was happy to walk home when he was done. We parked outside my mother's house. I studied the rose bushes my gramma loved. The buds were just peeking out, their pink tips emerging. Why would someone want them gone? It seemed like such a petty thing. Kandice and I walked the little path and up the steps. Before we could knock, my gramma opened the door and greeted us.

"What a surprise!" she said. "Come in before you let all the smoke smell into the house."

We stepped inside, received our hugs, and followed her into the kitchen, where my mom was cleaning up teacups on the little round table.

"Molly," my gramma hollered, "don't put the tea up, the girls are here."

My mother poked her head out of the kitchen. With a wide smile on her face, she asked, "Do you want tea? It's still warm."

"Sure, why not?" I smiled. Hugging my mom, I asked, "How was your tea with Margery?"

"It was good enough," my gramma huffed, settling into her chair, motioning for us to sit. "But I still feel like there's something up. She brought this woman named Heather with her," she added. "Some attorney. Said she's reviewing all of the land laws and insurance requirements. Making sure the historic district is compliant." My gramma wrinkled her nose. "I didn't like her."

"Now, Mom, we just barely met her. How can you not like somebody you just barely met?" my mother chirped while pouring Kandice and me tea.

"Thank you," Kandice acknowledged my mom. "Oh, that's easy. I don't like lots of people I meet for the first time."

"You make it sound like you're so mean," I said, laughing, adding creamer and honey to my tea.

"There is nothing mean about you, sweetie," my mother said to Kandice. She reached over and squeezed her hand.

"So what is it about this woman you didn't like, Gramma?" I asked, handing Kandice the honey.

"Oh, something just felt off about her. Margery can be stuffy. You know that. But this woman felt sharp, edgy like."

"Oh yes, I know Margery can be stiff," I said. "I was at the fairgrounds yesterday to check in with her, and she wasn't going to let me in to see people. She knows me. She knows I wasn't there to cause trouble."

My mother piped up. "She was just following whatever orders she was given."

My mother wanted to see the good in everyone. I did too, but sometimes you have to draw the line.

"It's one thing not to let suspicious people inside a shelter. It's another thing entirely not to let a town member you know come in," I grumbled. Turning back to my gramma, "What did she say about your bushes?"

"Well, it looks like they can't force her to remove them yet," my mother answered for her, taking a sip of tea.

"They're definitely not going anywhere," my gramma added firmly. "I'll stand outside in front of those bushes all day long if I have to."

My mother rolled her eyes. Gripping her teacup, she blew out a sigh. "Margery believes we will get to keep them because we have the original photographs showing they were there when the house was built. The historical society tries to keep everything as accurate as possible."

My gramma interrupted my mom, "She said if I kept them trimmed nicely, which we do, there probably wouldn't be a problem."

"Heather said she would do some checking into it," my mom continued. "She said she's going over a lot of the zoning in the area and making sure everything is compliant for the insurance companies."

"Do you know where she's from?" Kandice asked. "Do you know who she is?"

"Well, she's not local. I know that much," my mom said. "But it sounds like they're opening a local office here, so maybe she plans on staying. She didn't really say."

"Did Margery just bring her over without asking?" I asked, blowing on my tea to cool it.

My gramma snorted. "She did. Didn't say a word ahead of time. Just showed up with her like it was the most normal thing in the world. I was completely sideswiped. That's why I don't like her."

I furrowed my brows in thought. One, that didn't sound like my gramma because she usually loved people dropping by. But two, bringing an attorney to afternoon tea was strange.

"Kandice, honey, what have you been up to?" my mother asked, changing the subject. "We haven't seen you in a few weeks." She patted Kandice's arm.

"I've been buried in schoolwork," Kandice said with a smile. "Keeps me pretty busy."

"Did this Heather give you a business card or anything?" I asked, steering the conversation right back to the attorney.

"No," my mom said. "She didn't give us anything. They just came, had tea, and it was a perfectly nice conversation until we talked about the bushes. Once that subject came up, they didn't stay much longer."

"What exactly did she say?" I asked.

My gramma leaned back, thinking. "Well," she said slowly, "she told us the historic district was going to be reviewed very carefully."

My mother nodded. "She said something about how towns like ours sometimes have to make adjustments."

"What kind of adjustments?" Kandice asked.

My gramma shrugged.

"Heather said," my mother paused, trying to remember the exact words. "progress sometimes requires a few difficult changes, but it's always for the greater good of the community."

"That seems to be the theme around here," I said, taking a sip of my tea. "Hey, has Dad mentioned anything about Ryan or the military?" I asked. "He's always hanging out at the VFW. Has anything been going on down there?"

"Nothing specific," my mother said. "But the whole town feels uneasy. The military group up on the mountain, the fires, the insurance issues. There's just so much happening right now."

Kandice squeezed a little more honey into her tea and stirred vigorously.

"But now that you mention it," she added, "there was a guy your dad was talking to. He mentioned some corporation."

"What was it called?" she asked my gramma.

"Onyx... Ebony... something like that," my gramma muttered. "Oh, confounded. I can't remember," she said, balling her fist up in frustration.

"What was he saying about them?" I asked.

"He said word around the military guys is that some company has an interest in the valley, so they hired people to come in and observe the situation," my mom continued.

"And you can't remember the name?" I pressed.

"I've got it!" my gramma exclaimed. "Obsidian. That's what it was. I knew it was something black." She smiled.

"Did Margery or Heather mention anything about Obsidian?" I asked.

"No," my mother said. "From what I understood, Heather was here to review land use documents, historic district rules, and make sure everything worked for both homeowners and the insurance companies."

I laughed. "I don't think you can use those two things in the same sentence."

My mother frowned at me. "Why are you asking all of these questions? You girls aren't getting into trouble again, are you?" She eyed us.

"Nope," we said in unison.

"I wanted to know what the verdict on the bushes was. Don't worry, Detective David Parker is looking into the murder." I smiled.

"I just wanted to say hi," Kandice added.

We chatted a while longer before Kandice and I finally had to leave. I still had dinner tonight to get ready for, and the afternoon had already gotten away from me.

"I don't like that an attorney was here," I said once we were back in Kandice's car.

We pulled away from the curb and headed down the quiet street.

"Something seems off about that," Kandice agreed. "Why would Margery feel the need to bring her along? She's had tea with your family before."

"She's been head of the historical society for years. If she wanted to smooth things over about the bushes, she could've easily come by herself and pacified my gramma without dragging some attorney along," I said, leaning back in my seat.

"That's exactly what I was thinking," Kandice said, turning the corner towards my house.

"You know something else that's weird?" I added.

"What's that?"

"Rosie was all concerned about Ryan when everything started. Now Reed's been found dead, and we haven't heard a word from her."

"Maybe she's talked to Ryan? We did," Kandice suggested.

"Maybe," I hesitated. "I think I will give her a call. Her name wasn't on the shelter list. But she told me that's where she was staying."

I pulled out my phone and scrolled through my recent calls until I found Rosie's name. I tapped it and held the phone to my ear.

It rang a couple of times before she answered.

"Oh, hi Taryn," Rosie said, her voice very cheery. "I was just talking to Alex."

"Oh," I said, a little sharper than I meant to. "You were talking to Alex?"

Kandice shot me a quick look.

Rosie had been flirting with Alex since the beginning of all this. Hearing that she was chatting with him didn't surprise me.

"Yeah," Rosie replied casually. "We were just talking."

"About what?" I asked.

"Oh... you know." She paused. "Everything that's been going on. Everyone here at the fairgrounds is getting antsy."

"The fairgrounds?" I repeated. "I was at the fairgrounds, and you weren't there."

"I was out," she said, brushing the statement off. "Alex stopped by for a minute. We were just talking about how sad Reed's death is."

"Sad? I thought you didn't like him because he was pressuring Ryan to sell," I questioned her.

"Well, of course it is," Rosie said quickly. "Nobody deserves to die like that."

There was a brief pause on the line.

"Though I suppose when people start digging around in things that don't concern them... trouble tends to follow."

I leaned forward in the passenger seat, repositioning myself.

"What do you mean by that?" I asked.

"Oh, nothing," Rosie said quickly. "Just small-town talk, I guess."

I exchanged a glance with Kandice.

"Well, if you talk to Alex later, tell him I said goodbye. He had to run before we finished our conversation," she said in a playful voice and disconnected.

I wasn't sure why, but that bothered me more than it probably should have.

"Rosie seemed strange," I said, turning to Kandice. "Almost like she was hiding something, but I couldn't say what for sure."

"Did she say anything about Ryan?" Kandice asked.

"No, which is weird," I replied.

"Just add it to the list of strange behavior around here," Kandice smiled. "This smoke is getting to everyone's heads."

Chapter 17

Kandice had dropped me off, Alex was with David following up on yet another fire lead, and Robert came in from running his errands with a dress suit zipped inside a garment bag and a gift bag in his other hand.

"Here." he held up the bag and smiled. "I got you something to wear tonight."

"I didn't need you to get me anything to wear. I have plenty of things to wear," I said, accepting the gift hesitantly.

"I know, but I was out getting ready for dinner tonight, and I wanted you to have the perfect dress and shoes."

I looked at the bag again.

"You went shopping for a dress and shoes for me?" I asked, raising my eyebrows.

"Of course. I'm taking you to the fanciest place in Silver Springs. Just open the bag." He tapped the bag, his grin getting bigger.

I placed the bag on the dining room table. Reaching in, I pulled out an emerald-green slip dress that was slit up one side. I gasped. It was silk, so thin and cool to the touch, it felt like water sliding through my fingers. Holding it up, it weighed almost nothing.

"That's one hundred percent silk. It's meant to feel like you're wearing nothing." He smirked.

"This is way too much," I said. "I don't need this. I can't accept this."

"You will accept it," he replied calmly, "because that's how you're going as my date tonight."

I looked back inside the bag. There was a pair of silver strappy stilettos nestled in tissue paper, and at the bottom sat a small jewelry box. When I opened it, I found a delicate silver waterfall necklace and a matching pair of elegant teardrop earrings.

Turning back to Robert, I shook my head. "You know I can't accept this," I said. "You know we're not dating, and you know this is not a date."

"Taryn," he said softly, "I know we're not dating. I know you love Alex. And I know this isn't a date."

He paused and smiled gently.

"But what you don't know, is that I will love you forever, whether that be in the form of a friendship or a relationship. And these are for you because you will be my date tonight." He smiled.

I stepped forward and hugged him.

"Thank you," I said quietly, and I went to get dressed.

When I came out of my room wearing the outfit Robert had picked out, I felt a little like royalty. He was right about the dress. It felt like wearing nothing at all. It was the softest fabric I had ever touched.

Robert looked incredibly handsome in his suit. It molded to his chiseled chest. His tie and pocket square matched my emerald dress perfectly.

He offered his arm. "Shall we?" he asked.

"We shall," I said, taking it.

"You look beautiful, by the way."

"Thank you. You look good as well."

We took his red Corvette. As we left the town behind and started up the winding mountain road towards Alpine 85, Silver Springs' ski resort, the lights below grew smaller. The Sterling Elk came into view. Its wide glass windows cast a soft golden glow down the slope, like a beacon tucked into the mountainside.

A life-size silver elk statue stood at the entrance, shining beneath the evening lights. The restaurant sat on the edge of a mountain peak, overlooking the canyon.

The dinner reservation was made in his name, Robert Campbell. Weird that it wasn't under Oliver Thompson. Looks like Robert still has more pull than a councilman. Doesn't surprise me. Robert has a lot of pull wherever he goes.

Inside, the dining hall was framed by a massive wall of glass. The maître d' escorted us to a table along the far wall where the glass stretched from floor to ceiling. Sitting there felt like we were perched on the edge of the world. From our table, you could see the train tracks far below, cutting through the mountains towards Ironcrest.

I imagined how beautiful the view must be during winter snowstorms or when the fall leaves turned gold and red. Tonight was a bit eerie. The canyon below glowed orange from the fire still burning in the valley.

The restaurant balanced elegance and rustic mountain charm perfectly.

Black tablecloths covered the tables. Silver chargers and silver-stemmed wine glasses gleamed beneath the soft lighting. The floors were solid cherry wood, and the ceiling beams were thick wooden trusses. Tongue-and-groove walls held silver sconces that cast warm light across the room. A massive river rock fireplace stretched across nearly half of the wall to the right of the room.

Small silver elk figurines decorated little alcoves carved into the walls, and each table held a candlelit centerpiece: white vases streaked with silver veins, much like the veins seen in the mines.

Robert ordered the wine special for the evening while we waited for Councilman Thompson and his wife to arrive. The waitstaff had just finished pouring our wine when the Thompsons appeared.

Councilman Thompson was a big, boxy man with dark hair. He wore a black suit and a red tie. His wife, Amy, wore a sapphire-blue wrap dress that matched her eyes. Her blond hair was pulled back into a French twist. We stood to greet them.

"Councilman Thompson," Robert said. "This is my date, Taryn."

"Nice to meet you," I said, shaking his hand.

"And this is my wife, Amy," he said.

We all sat.

"You're the woman who solved the Crystal Lakes murder last fall," Thompson said. His tone was a bit hostile.

"Well," I said awkwardly, "I sort of did. If getting kidnapped counts." I half smiled.

Robert came to my rescue before the councilman could say anything else.

"Oliver," he said, "I invited you tonight because I have a few city planning questions. As you know, I've been attending the council meetings. We don't always agree, but I'd like to know how progress is going. It's my understanding that an expansion packet has been filed. I'd like to know if that includes my property as well."

I thought we were going to have to say a few more things first, maybe some idle chitchat, before Robert jumped into business. But Councilman Oliver Thompson did set the temperature with the Crystal Lakes comment. Interesting, I thought.

Amy sat quietly beside her husband, her eyes darting around the room. She hadn't spoken since we sat down. I could tell she knew something.

"You have nothing to worry about with your house, Robert," Oliver said. "You've seen the plans. The expansion packet doesn't go anywhere near your property. It encompasses the KOA campground and the surrounding area." He leaned back in his chair. "Outside counsel has been helping the town navigate the zoning process. A sharp woman. Knows her land law."

"Who is she?" I asked.

"Heather Katz and Marco Salgner. They represent the expansion interests. We just want to be sure everybody has proper coding and zoning. This is about future growth and development for Silver Springs. There's nothing wrong with that." He said smugly.

I continued watching Amy's face while her husband talked. She tried to plaster a smile on, like she agreed with everything he was saying, but it didn't reach her eyes. Something wasn't right. I needed to get her alone.

"The KOA campground is not that far from my place. How do I know you're not coming after my section of the valley? I mean, we do have to protect our interests, do we not?" Robert huffed.

Oliver frowned.

"You won't get me to say I'm benefiting from this or anything of the sort," he said. "I have a civic duty. It's my job to protect Silver Springs and ensure that it has the proper planning for growth."

"Oliver," I interrupted, "how do you feel about the Moon Map?"

He rolled his eyes in disgust.

"I think it's ridiculous," he said. "I don't know how that man's butt got so famous, and I have no idea why the city has encouraged it by putting it on the website. I really should speak to whoever handles our web development."

"I actually think it's quite funny," I said with a smile. "It seems to be bringing in tourists. Honestly, it's good for the town, and you just said you want to do what's best for the town."

Amy was still sitting quietly, still looking absolutely petrified.

"You know, Oliver," Robert added, "the map isn't a bad marketing plan. Jason does make the best moonshine in the valley, and I know several little shops sell his jars."

"Oh yes," Thompson said quickly. "Of course, we support local businesses here. That's never going to change. We simply need room to grow." He looked directly at me. "He does bring tourists, but is that the caliber of tourist we want, is the real question."

I tilted my head slightly. "I think our tourists come here for the mountains, for the train, for nature, for the campground, for the quirky little shops and the homemade trinkets. They come here for an escape," I said. My heart felt a little full thinking about the little town I loved so much. "And doesn't the Moon Map count as an adventure?" I added.

Amy finally spoke.

"That's true," she said softly. "You couldn't have said it more beautifully. Our town is a place to escape. It's about nature. We haven't forgotten that... right?"

She looked at her husband and gently patted his arm.

"Oh no, of course not. I would never want to imply that I wouldn't want locals and their artisans to be here, or that we would ever be anything but a beautiful mountain escape town. I think we got off on the wrong foot. I think we misunderstood each other." He smiled like the Cheshire Cat.

"Oh, good," Robert said. "I agree. I just wanted to see how things were going."

We sat silently, sipping our wine.

"It's a real shame what happened to Reed Jackson," I said, interrupting the silence and watching Amy carefully.

Her eyes grew wide. She nodded quickly. "Yes... it is."

"Did you know him very well?" I asked.

"Well... sort of," Amy answered. "I just started working at Suds and Scrubs."

I watched Councilman Thompson squeeze her hand, and she paused.

"And I think I cleaned his house a couple of times. I just met him." Her answer shortened real fast.

"Oh, so you guys didn't know him very well?" I questioned.

"He did come to several council meetings," Robert added.

Oliver looked back and forth between us.

"I don't know what either of you are implying," he said stiffly, "but I knew Reed no better than either of you. Whatever this conversation is about, I don't have answers for you."

The server cleared his throat politely.

"Good evening. May I tell you about our specials tonight?"

He began describing the evening's offerings while we glanced through the menus. The steaks were clearly the star of the night, along with several Colorado-inspired dishes: green chili roasted potatoes, grilled mountain vegetables, and smoked trout appetizers.

Robert and Oliver both ordered ribeye steaks. I chose the Hatch green chile crema gnocchi, and Amy had the elk medallion in a wild mushroom sauce. We placed our orders, and the conversation shifted into safer territory while we waited.

When the server returned with our meals, he carefully placed each plate in front of us.

Robert lifted his wine glass. "A toast," he said with a small smirk. "To Councilman Thompson and his progressive efforts to preserve Silver Springs' past while guiding it into the future."

We all raised our glasses. The conversation after that turned noticeably colder. Mostly idle chatter. Comments about the weather, how unusual all this rain has been for Colorado this time of year. Things like that. About halfway through the meal, Amy said she needed to use the restroom. She excused herself and got up.

I knew it was my chance. Hopefully, Oliver wouldn't think something was up, so I waited a couple of minutes before deciding I needed to use the restroom too. Inside the bathroom, I closed the door and locked it so nobody else could come in.

Amy stepped out of the stall and jumped slightly when she saw me.

"Oh! I didn't see you there, Taryn."

"Amy," I said gently, "I need to ask you a question." I wanted to cut to the chase.

She froze.

"It seemed to me you were very upset about Reed for someone who barely knew him."

"Oh... I just cleaned his house a few times," she said nervously. "It's just sad when somebody goes missing and then you find out they're dead. I mean, it's a horrible thing."

"Oh yes, it's horrible. But I get the feeling there's more to you being upset."

"Why would you think that?"

"It's just that when I was asking about him, you looked like you were about to cry. And when you told me you worked for Suds and Scrubs, you seemed to get tense and cut that conversation short. Are you sure everything's alright? Because you can tell me."

Amy broke down in tears.

"Oh, Taryn, I needed to tell someone. I've been so upset about what happened to Reed. He was just the nicest friend to our family. He's done so much for Oliver. He's helped his career in so many ways. And he did a lot for Suds and Scrubs too." She sniffled.

"I don't know if you know this, but because he was my friend, I was able to get all of Neighborhood Integrity's accounts to Suds and Scrubs. Anytime a Neighborhood Integrity agent rents a house, Suds and Scrubs gets the cleaning contract. Anytime there's a claim and construction done, Scrubs gets the cleaning contract. It's just so good for the community. Everything we did was good for the community."

I frowned slightly. "How did you know he was missing to report him? And what were the financial documents you mentioned were missing?" I asked.

Her eyes widened. "How do you know it was me who turned him in missing?" she asked.

"The report says an employee of Suds and Scrubs called him in missing," I said. "Wasn't that you?"

She nodded but didn't answer out loud. Her eyes darted around. She looked like she was trying to come up with an answer.

"Oh." She wrinkled her brow in thought. "I had seen a folder on the countertop when I was cleaning the house, and it wasn't there. It said, um, 'Finance' on it. So I just assumed with the folder missing and him missing that maybe he took them somewhere and got lost or was kidnapped. You know, who knows what. But I was just concerned because I hadn't seen him in a couple of days. That's all," she stammered.

I eyed her suspiciously. Her story felt flimsy. Like a piece of Swiss cheese, way too many holes in it, and stinky.

"Why do you want to know all this, Taryn?" she finally asked.

"My boyfriend is a private investigator, and he was hired to investigate one of the properties out in the valley. Reed's name has come up several times, and I thought I'd ask if you were the one who reported him missing and if you knew anything. Then I can report back to my boyfriend and let him know if I found anything out for his case," I lied. I was getting so good at lying. I needed to go to confession after this. Every time I investigate, I become a bigger liar. I said a quick prayer for myself.

This time she eyed me suspiciously. "Well, you know that he and I were just friends and that he did a lot for my husband and me, and for Suds and Scrubs by getting them those accounts. It's very helpful. He was a nice guy. It's always sad when somebody you know dies." She flipped the lock and exited the bathroom.

I took a deep breath before following her out. She was clearly hiding something. Councilman Thompson knew more than he let on, and she knew more too.

When I got back to the table, the server was bringing the dessert tray around. I decided to order the chocolate layer cake with raspberry filling and Chambord ganache. It looked divine.

We continued the rest of our evening with idle chitchat, but right when we were about to leave, Councilman Thompson left with a warning.

"Bye, Robert. Thank you again for the dinner. I trust I will see you at another council meeting soon." He smiled, looking at me, then back to Robert again. "That is, of course, unless you get bored with it."

Directing his attention to me, "Taryn, it was nice to meet you. Sorry you had such an unfortunate event last fall. I don't know how you can continue to ask so many questions after experiencing what you did." He smiled a wicked smile as he grabbed his wife's hand, and they left.

Robert escorted me out to his Corvette. Standing there in my thin silk dress beside his suit and tie, I smiled.

"That felt very James Bond-ish."

"Well, if James Bond is who I am, then we're off to a one-night stand next," he said. Then he paused. "Don't worry. Alex can have you back after we've had our Bond moment." He smirked.

"You had to go and ruin it, didn't you?" I laughed. "We have learned to have fun together again, though, haven't we?"

"Yes, we have." He kissed me on the top of the head and opened the door for me. Sliding into the seat, he drove me home.

Chapter 18

Robert and I walked into the house laughing. Alex and Kandice were sitting at my dining room table with a box of pizza, a couple of beers, and a box of donuts on the counter. Their dinner had clearly been very different from ours.

"Taryn," Alex said, standing as we came in. "You look breathtaking."

"Thank you." I smiled, spinning in a circle.

He grabbed me by the waist and kissed me. He whispered naughty stuff into my ear and I smiled. "If only we were alone," I whispered in reply.

Robert cleared his throat. "Okay, the dress was for me."

"It doesn't look like it." Kandice laughed.

Letting go of me, Alex asked, "How did the meeting go?"

"We didn't learn a lot," I said, slipping off my heels. "But Councilman Thompson is definitely hiding something. His wife, too. She acted like maybe she wasn't the one who reported him missing or that she was told to do it. Something was off."

Alex exchanged a glance with Kandice.

"Detective Parker confirmed Reed was murdered. Just like we suspected," Alex said.

"How?" I asked.

"Blunt force trauma to the head," Kandice said.

"So someone killed him... and then dragged him a thousand yards?" Robert asked.

"That's what it looks like so far," Alex replied.

"And Trey called," Kandice added. "The fire is forty percent contained. He should be back in town soon."

Robert frowned. "Interesting," he said slowly. "Now that Reed's been found, and the fire is partially contained... they're just leaving?"

No one had an answer. We ended up sitting around the table for what felt like hours, going over everything we'd figured out so far. By the time we finished, I was exhausted.

"I'm done," I finally said, pushing back from the table. "I'm going to bed."

The boys agreed. Kandice had already left earlier to take care of her dog, Fluffy. Alex and I were brushing our teeth and getting ready for bed when I heard a knock at the front door.

Robert hollered, "I'll get it," and headed for the door.

A moment later, I smelled burning cow poop. I rushed out of the bathroom with my toothbrush still in my hand. Alex was on my heels.

"Fire!" Robert shouted. "There's a fire on your doorstep."

He lunged forward and lifted his foot like he was about to stomp it out.

"Wait!" I screamed. "What are you doing?"

He froze.

"That's a flaming bag of cow poop!" I said.

His foot was inches away from smashing it.

I watched in horror, "You've never seen that before?" I asked.

"Apparently not," Robert muttered.

"Quick, get some water!" I said.

Alex ran to the kitchen and came back with a glass of water. He dumped it over the flaming bag on my front porch. The flames sputtered and died.

We stepped outside and looked around. No one. No note. No sign of anyone. Just a dilapidated bag of charred cow poop sitting on my doormat.

"Great," I sighed. "Now my doormat's ruined. And I liked that one too. It said, 'Welcome Spring!', with little tulips and butterflies. Now it's covered in charred cow poop." I closed the door with both boys staring at me.

"Shouldn't we clean that up now?" Alex asked.

"Nope," I said. "We'll clean it up tomorrow. It'll still be there waiting. I'm tired, and I'm going to bed. I can't worry about this today. I'll worry about it tomorrow."

The boys looked completely confused. This was unlike me. Normally, I would have cleaned it up immediately. But honestly, I was tired and over it. The cow crap could wait. I locked the door, grabbed Alex's hand, and pulled him towards the bedroom.

"Goodnight, Robert, " I hollered over my shoulder.

We climbed into bed and I was just about to pull the covers over my head when my phone rang.

It was my mom. Her calling this late at night couldn't be good. My heart started racing.

"Mom? Is everything okay?" I answered.

"There's been a fire, honey. But everyone's fine," she quickly added.

"There's been a fire?" I asked. My mouth went dry.

"Yes. Your grandmother's rose bushes caught fire."

"Oh my gosh! Is the house okay?"

"I believe so."

"What happened?"

"I don't know. We were all in bed when we heard shouting. We looked out the window and saw flames."

I could hear my mom take a deep breath.

"Jason Moon came by, alerting us. He grabbed our hose and started putting the fire out immediately."

"Wait," I said. "Did you say, Jason Moon?"

"Yes. Jason Moon. You know, the moonshine guy you and your brother went to school with?"

"I know who Jason Moon is," I said flatly. "Why was he outside your house?"

"I don't know." Mom continued. "He said he was walking by when he saw the flames. If it weren't for him, the house might have burned."

"What about Gramma's roses?"

"We don't know yet. We'll have to see in the morning."

My heart sank. Gramma would be devastated if they were gone.

"Mom... what did Jason say to you?"

"I don't know, honey. It all happened so fast. Your father ran downstairs and called the fire department. Jason was already out there spraying the bushes."

"Your grandfather ran outside so fast he didn't even have time to put his teeth in." She laughed softly.

I smiled despite myself. "Do you want me to come over?"

"No, honey. We're okay. I probably shouldn't have called you and scared you. With everything going on lately... I just felt uneasy."

"I'll be there first thing in the morning," I said. "Don't touch anything. Let Alex look at it."

"Okay, honey. I love you."

"I love you too."

We hung up. I turned to Alex. "My grandmother's rose bushes were just on fire. And Jason happened to be there to put them out."

Alex frowned. "Your gramma's house catches fire at the same time you get flaming crap on your doorstep," he said. "That's a message. This is no accident."

Robert appeared in the doorway, entered my room, and sat on the edge of the bed. "I couldn't help but overhear," he admitted.

"You were listening." I smirked.

He smiled, "And I agree with Alex. This is a threat. It's not a coincidence that both your house and your parents' house got a little fire tonight. You've poked the beehive," he said. "The question is... who's the hornet?"

I didn't sleep well the rest of the night. All I could think about were the conversations we'd had that day. Jason. Brandon. Rosie. My mother. Margery. Robert and my dinner with the Thompsons. So many people could be involved.

But why? Why attack my gramma's rose bushes? Why leave flaming cow poop on my doorstep? The thoughts swirled around in my head.

When I woke up, I was grumpy and exhausted. The boys were already up, making coffee and breakfast, when I stumbled into the kitchen.

"Good morning, sunshine," Robert said with a grin, handing me a cup of coffee.

"I don't feel like it's a very good morning," I muttered, but I accepted the coffee, grateful for it.

Alex kissed me on the cheek. "I assume you didn't sleep well."

"Nope. Did you?" I asked.

"Nope," Alex grumbled.

"Me neither," Robert added. "I was wide awake on the couch half the night waiting for someone to break in and try to kill you."

I stared at him. "Dramatic much?"

Before he could reply, there was a knock at the door.

"Great," I groaned. "Now what?" I said, heading to open the door.

Kandice stood on the porch.

"Do you know you have cow crap on your front porch?" she asked.

"Yes," I sighed. "I'm aware."

She stepped over it, coming inside. "What happened last night?"

"It was a real party," I sighed. "Someone torched my gramma's rose bushes and left me a flaming pile of cow poop. Apparently, I have made somebody mad, and I guess they think it's funny to light poop on fire and ruin my door-mat."

Kandice burst out laughing. "That's because it is funny."

"There is nothing funny about this," I said.

"Oh yes, there is," she said between giggles. "You always have the strangest things happen to you."

"If you like flaming cow poop so much, feel free to take it home with you," I said, probably a little too grumpily to my best friend.

Kandice just laughed harder.

We sat down at the table to figure out what to do next.

"I promised my mom I'd stop by this morning with Alex to look at the scene," I said.

Kandice glanced at the clock. "I have class in an hour. Unfortunately, I cannot be of much help. But I have always wanted to leave flaming crap on someone's doorstep. Once you figure out who did this, let's return the favor." She smiled.

"Hey, Robert. Since you are free this morning, can you do me a favor?" I asked.

He narrowed his eyes. "Why do I get the feeling this is something I'm not going to want to do?"

"You're not," I admitted. "But I need you to go see Angie."

"Nope," he said immediately. "Absolutely not. She won't talk to me anyway."

"If you don't want awkward encounters, stop sleeping with half the women in this town." Kandice laughed.

"Hello, pot, have you met the kettle?" Robert snapped.

"You're right," I said, "She probably won't want to talk to you, but she likes the chocolate-filled croissants," I said sweetly. "Go apologize for your behavior and see what she can dig up on Jason's liquor license."

He groaned. "I don't need poop on my doorstep, too," he protested.

Chapter 19

When Alex and I pulled up to my mother's house, Scotty was already there.

A small crowd had gathered in the front yard, everyone standing in a loose circle around the rose bushes. Or what was left of them.

My stomach sank. Please let one survive, I prayed as we walked up the path. My gramma stood near the garden with tears in her eyes. Blackened branches stuck out of the soil like skeleton fingers, and the once-beautiful bed of roses looked like someone had taken a blowtorch to them.

I threw my arms around my gramma, "Gramma, I'm so sorry about your rose bushes."

"It's not your fault, honey," she said softly, patting my arm.

But I wasn't so sure about that. I could've very easily upset the killer, and this is probably a warning to back off.

My grandfather and my dad were already surveying the damage, bending down and poking through the charred remains. Scotty was crouched nearby, snapping pictures with his phone.

"I called my fire inspector," Scotty said when he noticed us. "He's coming over as soon as he can. Figured I'd start documenting things in case anything changes."

Alex knelt near the edge of the flower bed and studied the ground carefully. After a moment, he pointed to something small in the dirt.

"This looks like part of a paper bag," he said.

Scotty leaned down beside him and snapped another photo. The tiny scrap was brown and crumpled. I felt a sinking feeling in my stomach.

"There was a bag of flaming cow poop on your sister's porch last night," Alex whispered.

Scotty looked up at me slowly. His expression had turned serious. "She didn't mention that earlier."

"It happened right before your mother called about the fire," Alex explained.

Scotty frowned. "Coincidence?" he asked.

"I would think not," Alex replied. "It ruined her doormat." Alex stood up, brushing dirt off his hands. "I'm calling Detective Parker," he said. "He's working the homicide case, but maybe he can stop by here, too," Alex suggested. "He should probably see this."

"Good idea," Scotty agreed.

My dad looked from one of them to the other. "Are you saying someone may be threatening our family?"

Alex and Scotty exchanged a glance before answering. "We think so."

My grandfather shuffled over from the crowd of spectators. "That's it," he declared. "I'm going down to the V and calling in the troops."

My mother blinked. "What troops?"

"The VFW," Grandpa said proudly. "Nobody messes with my family and gets away with it. We're trained military professionals."

My grandmother sniffed. "You're also almost eighty years old," she added.

The two of them immediately started bickering about whether or not the VFW was going to conduct a full tactical operation in the front yard. Alex stepped aside and called David while I confessed to my parents what had happened at my place. I could see my mother's urge to start cleaning something emerging. I think she was beginning to twitch.

"David said he's on his way to the station," Alex reported a moment later. "He'll swing by here first."

Alex turned to me, "He said to tell you, don't touch anything."

I rolled my eyes. "I never touch anything. Why does everyone keep saying that to me?"

By the time Detective Parker arrived, half the neighborhood had gathered in my parents' front yard.

The gossip mill was working overtime. Neighbors whispered in small groups while staring at the burnt rose bushes as if it were the morning's entertainment. I heard rumors that my gramma probably made Margery mad. The neighbors listened intently to both of my grandparents' stories.

"I had to run outside without my teeth!" my grandpa said dramatically. "There was no time to save them, and now I am calling in the troops. No one threatens my family and gets away with it!" he declared.

The neighbors gasped. My gramma was telling everyone, "This is what happens when you stand up for yourself." We have to be strong. My parents sat quietly on the porch steps, holding hands, both looking exhausted, worried, and unwilling to rein in my grandparents. Then I spotted a familiar figure weaving through the crowd. Racheal Post, reporter for the Silver Springs Times.

Great, I knew she was going to want a comment. She spotted me immediately and hurried over.

"Oh, hi, Taryn!" she said, squeezing past the neighbors. "What happened? Do you think it was arson? Do you have a suspect?" Racheal fired off questions.

I knew whatever I said would be in tomorrow's paper. Then I thought this could be an opportunity to call out the killer.

"I have one thing to say," I replied.

Racheal leaned in eagerly.

"No one threatens my family and gets away with it."

Her eyes lit up. "So you think this was a threat?"

"I think something isn't right," I said evenly.

"Come on, Taryn," she pushed. "Just give the people of Silver Springs a little something."

I crossed my arms. "Now that we know the fires are connected..."

Before I could finish my threat to the killer or arsonist or both, a familiar voice cut through the crowd.

"Taryn." Detective Parker pushed his way through the group and grabbed my arm. "No more comments," he said quietly. "Come with me." He looked around at the others. "And grab your family. I don't want anyone else talking either."

We gathered everyone and headed inside the house. Once the door closed behind us, the crowd outside slowly began to scatter. Racheal lingered long enough to take a few pictures of the rose bushes before leaving. Detective Parker motioned for us to sit at the kitchen table.

"I don't want to alarm anyone," he began, "but I have reason to believe this may be connected to the fires in the valley... and Reed's murder."

The room went silent.

"We're putting together a list of people to question," he continued. "If any of you can think of someone who might want to send this kind of message to your family, now would be the time to say so."

He looked directly at me. "And Taryn."

"Yes?" I asked.

"I do not want you investigating this any further." He leaned forward. "And I do not want you speaking to reporters anymore."

"What? I haven't done anything," I protested.

Alex squeezed my hand under the table. That was his silent signal to shut up. Unfortunately, I recognized the signal because I used it on him all the time. So I shut my mouth and listened to David finish his lecture.

My mother, of course, had questions and was quickly becoming terrified. My grandmother, on the other hand, had already started compiling a list of people she could accuse of doing something like this. My grandpa was itching to get down to the VFW and was ready to start a war. My father just looked tired, worried, and angry all at the same time. I knew he was thinking the same thing Alex was thinking. How was he going to protect the women he loved?

I walked over and hugged my dad, kissing his cheek.

"It's going to be okay," I whispered.

"I know, sweetie," he said quietly.

The adrenaline from the morning was starting to wear off. Detective Parker eventually stepped outside with Alex and Scotty to continue examining the yard. I stayed inside with my family.

My grandfather pulled me aside. "What do you think is going on here?" he asked quietly.

I lowered my voice. "I think someone we talked to yesterday might be the killer."

Gramma leaned closer. "Margery?" she whispered.

"Maybe," I said. "But that doesn't completely make sense."

"It could be Heather," Gramma added. "I didn't like her from the beginning."

That was true. I doubted Ryan knew where my parents lived. Not that it would be hard to find an address these days. But burning my grandmother's rose bushes? That felt personal, deliberate, and that meant it would be someone close to us.

"Did anything unusual happen yesterday?" I asked.

Gramma shook her head. "Nope. It was a normal day. We did laundry, had coffee, and your mother made another batch of Irish muffins for tea. Your father and grandfather had lunch before they went golfing, since the sun had come out. Then you and Kandice came by. We had dinner and a quiet evening."

"Mom said Jason knocked on the door and put the fire out," I said.

"Yes, that's what happened," my mom replied.

"What are the odds of someone walking by at the exact moment a fire starts?" I asked.

Then she looked directly at me, her voice firm. "I don't believe Jason is involved. Just because he's a little quirky doesn't mean he runs around setting rose bushes on fire." She crossed her arms. "You heard Detective Parker. Leave it alone. He will figure out what's going on."

I felt myself starting to get annoyed, but I forced a smile onto my face. "Of course, Mom," I said sweetly.

Across the table, my gramma caught my eye. She looked at me and immediately knew what I was doing. She could see that I had my fingers and toes crossed behind my back. Gramma just gave me a little smirk.

Robert returned from his meeting with Angie just as Alex and I pulled up to the house.

"What did you find out?" I asked, hopping out of the truck.

"Angie's still a little mad at me, but I am taking her to dinner to make up for it."

"You are taking her to dinner?" I eyed him as we walked up the steps. Alex followed behind us.

"Not because I want to, but because I thought it would be the nice thing to do since you seemed upset with me for my behavior." He smirked.

I rolled my eyes, pulling my keys out to unlock the door. My poop melted mat had dried out from the cleaning, but the blackened, melted tulips looked so sad. "I didn't say you need-ed to take her on a date. I said you needed to apologize. I am almost always upset with your behavior." This time, I smirked.

"Nice job, Robert. Giving Angie the date she deserved is a good look for you." Alex patted Robert's back.

Robert shook his cooties off. "I am doing it for Taryn. I was a jerk in the past. I am trying to be the man she thought I was all along."

Robert took a seat at the table. "So, do you want to hear the scoop from Angie on Jason's liquor license or not?"

Alex and I took seats at the table as well. "Yes, we need to know how this plays into everything."

"Well, it's legit, nothing shady, but there's a twist." Robert smiled.

I raised an eyebrow. "A twist?"

"Yeah," he said. "He's got a temporary license for a property that technically doesn't exist yet."

"Is he opening another shop?" I asked, still a little confused.

"No, Jason secured the rights to sell alcohol at Camp World," Robert replied.

"Jason said he didn't know why Reed was harassing him, and Councilman Thompson was poking around his liquor license," Alex stated.

"Right, but he must have gotten ahead of them somehow," Robert suggested.

"Camp World doesn't even own anything in Silver Springs," I said.

"Not yet, but the state issued it, probably anticipating future operations," Robert pointed out.

I frowned. "Wait... so he can legally sell alcohol there... even though there's no Camp World?"

Robert nodded. "Exactly. And that's not all. While I was digging, I noticed he's listed as a managing partner at Obsidian. Totally legal, but unusual. That connection could give him a vested interest if Ryan sells to Camp World."

"Obsidian? That's the name being thrown around the VFW." I leaned forward. "So... he's protecting himself, or his investments, or both."

"Right." Robert leaned back in his chair. "He's got a reason to watch every move."

I sat back, running a hand through my hair. "Great. So Jason does know more than he's letting on."

"Looks like it," Robert agreed.

Giselle started meowing and dancing around the front door. This was weird since she was an indoor-only cat. We all looked at her as she stretched up, pawing at the doorknob. Glancing at the boys and then back to Giselle, I got up. "What is it, sweet baby?" I picked her up and nuzzled her. Peering through the peephole, I saw nothing. I went to my office. Looking out the window, I could see a vase of flowers sitting on my poop mat. "Someone left us flowers," I hollered to the boys.

Alex retrieved the flowers and the note accompanying them. I didn't need to read the note. The flowers said everything I needed to know. Wrapped in brown parchment paper, tied with twine, was a bundle of Torch Lilies, and neatly tucked into the middle was a Black Baccara Rose. The wildly creepy bouquet was rounded out with sprigs of Silver Dust and Smoke Bush plumes. I dropped into my dining table chair and sighed. "Really?"

Alex looked extremely unhappy with my gift. Setting it on the table, he removed the note. It was sealed in red candle wax with the letter R. He took a picture of it before proceeding to open it. Robert and I sat on the edge of our seats waiting for Alex to read the threat.

Alex carefully opened the wax-sealed envelope, pulling out a charred piece of paper. It looked like the paper might have been torn into pieces, and we had received only one part of it. I could make out a large letter K, the letters rson, the word final.

"This is wonderful. Who received the rest of the gift, or am I supposed to receive more of these macabre bouquets?" I blew out a sigh.

I wasn't long before Detective Parker was at my table, giving me a stern look of disgruntled disbelief. He turned the paper over, examining it. We sat quietly, watching him intently as he examined the note and bouquet. He finally spoke, "This looks like a warning. Someone wants you to know enough but feel helpless. I am putting Officer Ballenger on this."

Pulling out his phone, he called him. Officer Ballenger had helped on the Crystal Lakes murder I was involved in last fall. I am sure he will be thrilled to find out I was involved in another one.

"Hey buddy, I need you to do me a favor. Can you look into the local flower shops and see if anyone ordered and delivered Torch Lilies today or this week?"

David paused while listening to Officer Ballenger on the other line.

"Yeah, I am hoping it won't take long. Check if any of the stores are carrying these flowers now as well."

"Okay, buddy, thanks." David disconnected. Addressing us, he said, "Officer Ballenger is tracking down where these flowers came from. There are only a couple of flower shops in town, so it shouldn't take long to find out if these came from one of them."

David stood. "I need to get back to the station and process all of this. Taryn, I don't have to tell you, but I don't like this. If Ryan contacts you, I need you to find out his location and let me know."

"You don't think he did this, do you?" I asked, a little worried that maybe he did.

"I can't be sure of anything at this point except that the killer or arsonist or both are now targeting you. Now I need to narrow down who wants to harm you."

Chills ran down my spine. Alex grabbed my hand and squeezed it tightly, and Robert grabbed my other hand. Both boys stiffened at David's words.

Chapter 20

Detective Parker left, and everyone was feeling a little uneasy. I started pacing the floor. I couldn't sit here and do nothing. I felt like my grandpa. I needed to call in the troops.

"That flaming death bouquet was a clue," I said. "The killer is playing a game of cat and mouse. I feel like there is something they want me to know." Still pacing, I announced, "I want to go confront Jason one more time. Maybe all he was really doing was protecting himself, and maybe he really was just walking by my parents' house. But we need to talk to him. I also feel like I need to corner Amy. I need to stop by Suds and Scrubs and see if she's working today."

"I don't love this, but I think you might be right," Robert said, standing from the table.

"I know I am right," I replied.

Alex remained seated at the table, arms crossed against his chest, staring at the bouquet. "We should give David a little bit of time. There is a chance he will know who sent this disaster by this afternoon." Alex gestured towards the flowers.

"Fine, let's eat lunch, give him a little time, then go question our own people," I relented.

Alex reluctantly agreed.

We heated up leftovers and sat at the table, pretending life was normal. As we were finishing, I got a phone call.

"Hello, Taryn O'Kelly speaking," I answered.

A voice on the other line whispered, "Taryn?"

"Yes. May I ask who is calling?"

"Um... this is Amy. Amy Thompson."

"Amy? What can I do for you?" I asked, a little surprised.

Both the boys looked up at me. I shrugged and put my hand in the air. I wasn't sure what was going on.

"Can you meet me at Penny's Coffee Shop?" Amy's voice was timid.

"Yeah, Penny's, sure. When?" I asked.

Robert started cleaning up the dishes with the anticipation that we might be going somewhere.

"It's just something you said last night that has been bothering me. I feel like I need to talk to you."

"Okay," I replied.

"But don't tell anyone. Don't bring anyone with you," she said quickly.

"Amy, what is this about?" I asked.

"I'll talk to you when we get to the coffee shop. Please don't tell anybody about this. If you bring anyone with you, I won't talk. I'll meet you in ten minutes."

She hung up.

I looked at the boys. "That was Amy Thompson. She wants me to meet her at Penny's Coffee Shop in ten minutes, and I'm not to bring anybody or tell anybody. She said something I said last night is bothering her."

Both boys eyed me.

"I don't like this," Robert said. "Something feels off. We just had dinner with her last night. If she wanted to confess something, she could've confessed then."

"Yeah," Alex added. "You get the death bouquet, and an hour later, Amy suddenly wants to talk to you. This doesn't feel right."

"I know. But what if she's telling the truth?" I asked.

"Well, we're coming with you then," Alex insisted.

"No, you can't. She said I could bring no one," I argued.

"We can't possibly let you go by yourself," Robert piped up.

"How about we compromise?" I said. "Robert, she knows you more than she probably knows Alex. How about you stay in the car and watch from the parking lot, and Alex, you come in after me and sit at your own table? That way, you're in the room, but it won't look like we're together. Alex's face isn't as familiar in town just yet. Everyone knows you, Robert."

"Fine. It's a plan. I'm not sure I like it, but it's a plan," Robert said.

"Agreed," Alex replied.

I grabbed my purse and keys, and we headed down the steps. At the driveway, I gave my keys to Robert. He would take my truck so he'd have a car to sit in. His Corvette was too flashy, and she'd probably recognize it.

It was a very short walk from my place to Penny's, so I walked ahead of Alex, hoping it didn't look suspicious. That way, he could keep his eyes on me.

Entering the shop, Amy wasn't there. I went to the counter and ordered a mocha latte. The barista gave me a little number to take to my table and told me she would bring the mocha out to me. I thanked her and found the corner table where Robert could see me through the window from the parking lot.

The barista, named Isabella, delivered my mocha. I was still waiting for Amy. She hadn't shown up. Isabella asked if I needed anything else. She had kind, large brown eyes and dimples when she smiled. I thanked her, but no. I told her that I was waiting for someone.

Moments later, Amy entered the shop. She placed her order and joined me at the table. I could see Alex entering after she sat down with me. He placed his order and grabbed a table in the opposite corner.

"Hi, Amy. What is it that you want to talk about?" I motioned for her to sit down.

She looked around. "You didn't bring anyone, did you?" she asked, sliding into her seat.

"No," I lied, "just me, like you asked. What is this about?" I smiled.

She saw Alex sitting in the corner and looked at me, then looked at him again. I was hoping she didn't realize he was with me. She looked back at me, leaned in, and whispered. "I didn't report Reed as missing."

"What? I thought you did. You work for Suds and Scrubs." I took a sip of my coffee, trying to act casual.

"I only work for Suds and Scrubs because I was asked to by my husband and Reed," she replied.

We paused as Isabelle brought Amy her tea.

"Thank you," Amy said.

"You're welcome." She smiled.

When she was no longer in earshot, I asked, "Why would Reed and your husband want you to take that job?"

"It was to secure accounts for Suds and Scrubs. Reed was doing something. I don't exactly know what." She took the lid off of her tea and blew on it. "Some big changes are coming to the valley, and my husband is involved in them. It is going to be good for his career. Securing accounts for a local business like Suds and Scrubs makes everything look so town-friendly. And it is," she sighed, "I had no choice but to take the job. They told me it was better for my husband's career."

Taking a long sip of coffee, I sat in thought for a moment before asking, "Then who reported him missing?"

"That's the thing. I think I know who, but I can't be certain. I think it was Heather Katz. The attorney who's been helping my husband with all the land documents. She worked with Reed a lot, too." Amy sipped her tea.

My stomach tightened.

"The day he went missing, Heather told me I needed to go clean his house. While there, I needed to look for a folder labeled finances. If I found it, I was supposed to bring it to her. She said they were partners, and she needed the documents for an expansion packet." She stared into her tea.

"And did you find it? You mentioned it was on the counter last night." I pressed.

"I didn't find a folder. I didn't find anything. Reed wasn't home. It was shortly after that the newspaper got notice that the Suds and Scrubs employee discovered financial documents missing and Reed missing. I was so nervous, I had to take the last few days off." Her eyes teared up.

"Why would they assume he was missing just because they sent you over to clean?" I questioned.

"I don't know. Everybody's been acting so weird lately, and I'm scared. I really did like Reed. He seemed like a nice guy. But with what everybody's saying about him in town, if he really was threatening people and possibly starting fires just to get insurance companies to not pay and to drop their clients, then that's just horrible."

"Do you believe your husband knows all of this?" I asked.

Amy hesitated, looking around the room. She made eye contact with Alex again and then looked back at me.

"Do you know that guy?" she asked, flicking her eyes in Alex's direction.

"If we're being honest, yes, I do know who he is. But you have nothing to worry about." I took a sip of my coffee.

Her eyes widened. "I said not to bring anyone."

"Amy, do you think your husband knows what's going on? Do you think your husband knows who killed Reed?" I pushed.

"I want to say no. I love my husband. He's never done anything like this before. He's driven, yes. He gets these intense visions that he just obsesses over. He has to accomplish them. But he's never been violent, and he's never been mean. So I know he didn't kill Reed. But I've never been sure if I actually liked Heather... and that other guy from her office. I only met him once."

She stood suddenly. "Taryn, I really need to go. I'm getting uncomfortable now. I'm afraid somebody's watching. I just don't know who."

She grabbed her tea and started to scurry off. I reached out and grabbed her.

"Wait, Amy. Thank you for being honest with me. We're going to get to the bottom of this. I have a couple more questions for you."

"I don't know, Taryn. I really shouldn't say anything else." She looked around the room once more.

"Please. My family has been threatened. If you know anything that can help us find out who the killer is, please?" I begged.

She sat back down. "What is it that you want to know?"

"Have you ever heard the name Obsidian?" I asked.

"I heard Heather mention it once. I have no idea what it is. I believe it's a company that employs her and Camp World. But I can't be certain."

"Thank you. What about Jason Moon or Ryan Newman? What can you tell me about them?"

"I know that Jason Moon has made my husband very angry. He thinks his mooning of the city is juvenile, and he wants his liquor license pulled. I don't know why he's so out to get him. He's never explained why he has such a hatred for him. But I do know they've fought a lot over the last several months."

"And Ryan?" I took another sip.

"All I know is that he didn't want to sell to Camp World. Both my husband and Heather felt like that would be best for the community. Other towns in Colorado report they've done so well with Camp World, and my husband believes it will help Silver Springs. But I guess Ryan's just not interested. That's really all I know. I do have to go."

She grabbed her tea and scurried off.

I sat there for a moment, thinking about what she had said, allowing her to leave. Alex did too.

My phone buzzed. "I see you are at Penny's. I just got done with class. I will swing by," it read. I texted Kandice back, letting her know I was already heading home, but to come on by and see my creepy bouquet. Then I proceeded to text her a picture of it.

A few moments later, Alex got up and approached me, joining me at the table.

"What did she say?" he asked, eyeing my phone.

"Let's grab Robert and go home, then I'll tell you," I said.

Alex and I piled into my truck with Robert behind the wheel.

"What did she want?" Robert questioned before I could close the door.

"She confessed she wasn't the one who reported Reed missing," I said.

"Then who did?" Alex asked.

"She doesn't know. That's the thing. She didn't even want to work at Suds and Scrubs. Her husband and Heather Katz talked her into it."

"Interesting," Robert muttered, pulling out of the parking lot. "I didn't see anyone suspicious out here. How about in there, Alex?"

"No, it was just us," Alex replied.

Entering the house, Robert placed my keys on the hook by the door. I walked straight to the dining table and dropped myself into a chair. The boys followed and took seats nearby. Kandice came in almost immediately behind us.

"What a hideously gorgeous threat," she said, pointing to the flowers.

"I know, it's thoroughly creepy, yet intriguing at the same time." I half smiled. "I was just telling them about Amy's confession."

"Back up." Kandice put her hand up. "You talked to Amy again? When?" she asked, joining us at the table, dragging the bouquet closer.

I brought Kandice up to speed. As I was filling her in, my eyes drifted to the hideous bouquet I'd been gifted. Something about the brown paper wrapping caught my attention.

"What is that?" I pointed to the paper wrapped around the bouquet.

"It looks burned," Kandice said.

I reached over and picked up the flowers. There was a tiny burned edge tucked inside the fold. I quickly grabbed the flowers and began unwrapping them. As I did, little torn pieces of burnt paper fell out. There was a large letter O. I immediately knew it was a puzzle, and the note was part of it. Kandice and I quickly began trying to assemble the message.

"Dang it. Detective Parker took the other pieces with him," I said, pointing. "But they fit here."

Alex was already pulling out his phone. He brought up the photo he'd taken earlier. The completed note read Kill Off Arsonist final notice.

"What the heck is that supposed to mean?" I questioned.

Alex snapped a few more pictures of the inside of the bouquet and sent a text to David. A moment later, his phone buzzed.

He read the message out loud. "The bouquet came from Buckets of Flowers Boutique downtown. A male placed the order and paid with cash. I'm headed to Jason Moon's shop to question him now."

We studied the image again, Alex's phone stuck into the burned-out space as though it were the missing piece of paper. The letters KOA stood out more and more the longer we looked at them.

"That's pointing directly to Ryan's property," I said finally. "We have to go back out there. We have to find Ryan. If he is the one doing these things, he needs to be stopped. If he's being set up, we need to save him. Either way, I've got to get out there."

I jumped up, reaching for my coat and keys, Kandice on my heels.

"Now the Angels are back!" she squeaked.

My phone rang. I sighed when I saw it was my mother. "The Angels are on pause," I said before answering the phone.

"Taryn, honey. I know you're busy, but your grandfather has declared war on whoever set your grandmother's rose bushes on fire. He's at the VFW right now recruiting anyone who can see in the dark. He's building his own civilian army. If you have a moment, can you go down there and please tell him to stop? Your grandmother and I have already tried. He won't listen to reason. And your father seems to be okay with it. He doesn't think at their age they can get into much trouble. Does he know this family?" My mother sighed.

I rolled my eyes. I loved my family. I really did. Taking a deep breath, I said, "Absolutely, Mom. I'll go down there and take care of it right now."

"Thank you, sweetie," my mom replied.

I disconnected and turned to my friends. "My grandpa's causing a ruckus, and we need to go stop him first."

They exchanged glances.

"The apple didn't fall far from the tree now, did it?" Alex said, grinning.

"Not funny," I snapped, stomping my foot.

"He's not wrong," Robert added, laughing

Kandice just laughed.

"Whose team are you on?" I argued. "Either you guys get your coats and come with me or stay here, but I've got to go deal with my grandpa."

We grabbed our things and headed out.

Chapter 21

It was a short drive to the VFW. The streets were dimmer now. This evening was settling in fast. A few storefronts were already shuttered, and the air carried that restless, waiting feeling the town seemed to have developed over the past few days.

When Alex pulled us into the parking lot, I noticed how packed it was, not just with pickups and sedans, but half a rolling military museum. World War II Jeeps sat crooked near the entrance. There was even an old olive-green transport truck, along with other well-kept classic military vehicles I didn't know the names for. The VFW looked like it had been called back into service after a very long retirement.

When we walked into the meeting hall, it was filled with at least twenty or thirty men well into their seventies. Many were wearing old military fatigues. A couple even had canes. I paused just inside the doorway, taking in the hodgepodge group. I had to smile, even though the whole thing felt utterly ridiculous. Here my grandfather was, putting together an army to keep our town and his family safe. It filled me with a strange mix of pride and worry.

The old VFW hall hadn't changed much since I was a kid. The wood-paneled chair rails and painted, fading yellow walls were lined with old flags and yellowing photographs. Framed newspaper clippings from long-forgotten wars still hung in the room, a testament to battles both terrifying and triumphant. Well-used, worn, folding chairs lined the walls. The low stage had American flag–style sashes swooping across the front, a microphone in the middle, and a podium waiting for the next speech. The air smelled faintly of coffee, whiskey, furniture polish, and dusty relics. A dented metal fan in the corner hummed loudly, its buzz barely competing with the energy in the hall. The room was full of stubborn old men reliving their youth, the greatest and most terrifying moments etched into their expressions.

I crossed the room, dodging men who were clearly eager to grab anyone within reach and launch into a war story. I spotted my grandfather at a table covered in maps of Silver Springs. Little plastic G.I. Joe figures were scattered across it.

He was motioning towards one of them, explaining his plan to another old friend standing beside him.

"Grandpa," I said, stepping in. "I'm sorry to interrupt, but Mom and Gramma sent me down here. They asked you to stop."

"Oh now, lass," he said without even looking up. "There's work to be done. We can't let this town be run over by arsonists and criminals. Those poor people in the evacuation zone are counting on us. Our military fellows are pulling out." He stomped his foot and raised his hand for emphasis.

"What do you mean? " I asked, furrowing my brow.

"Word on the military circuit is that a private analytics firm flagged unusual ignition clusters across the region. The report went through wildfire coordination channels, and the county requested temporary modeling and satellite support. Last I heard, there were a few anomalies that couldn't be fully explained, but command considers the fire contained well enough. They're pulling out. So it's our duty to step forward and protect this town. Our firefighting boys are still on the mountain. The winds have shifted. Your grandmother's rose bushes were under attack." he declared.

It took everything inside me not to laugh. But one part of what he said hit me like a sharp pain to the gut. If the military was leaving, if the threat was considered contained, Ryan's property would be vulnerable. The KOA. Final Notice. The killer was going to be there tonight. A chill ran through me.

"Grandpa," I said carefully, "I actually think I have something for you guys to do."

My mother was going to kill me.

"But I'm heading to the KOA in just a couple of minutes. I suspect something sinister is going down, and I could use a little backup."

"Yippee!" He actually skipped. "I knew my granddaughter was as clever as a crow at a wake. You heard her, boys! Roll 'em out!"

Robert and Alex rushed to my side.

"What have you done?" they asked in unison.

"Nothing. Just trust me. I think something is going down at the KOA, and I think we can use all the help we can get. Grandpa says the military's pulled out. The fire's not fully contained, but close enough. The threat clearly said KOA. Killed off arsonist. Final notice. I think there's a plan to kill someone there tonight."

The battalion leaving was something else. The scrape of folding chairs echoed as the old men shuffled out of the way, their boots scuffing, canes bumping with surprising urgency. Moments before, they had felt crowded and chaotic, but now they moved with purpose. Within minutes, we were outside, watching as the men poured into their vehicles, ready to relive their glory days. Engines roared to life, some smooth, some grinding. Headlights flickered on across the lot, casting long shadows. The transport truck even crop-dusted a large plume of black smoke that drifted above the military vehicles. I stood there for a moment, half-stunned, thinking about what all these men had been through, all they had seen. I couldn't help but be amazed at their courage and their ability to rally together when it was needed most.

It looked like a small convoy heading off to war, a parade of history rolling out to defend the town, refusing to give up without a fight.

Alex leaned into me, "You realize this could save the day or it could be a disaster, right?"

Robert shook his head, his expression serious. "Remind me never to mess with your grandpa, and I thought it was you I had to be scared of."

"Are you sure your grandpa isn't my grandpa?" Kandice smiled, "This is my kind of fun."

Grandpa climbed into his Jeep like a general heading into battle and waved us forward. "Move out!" he hollered, and just like that, away we went.

I didn't really want a bunch of seventy-plus-year-old men running around a trailhead, though I doubted they'd have much of a problem with it. If anything, they'd probably be excited. So instead of pulling into the lookout point parking where we had met Ryan, we turned onto County Road 253, heading to the KOA parking lot. The military really had pulled out. The camp, once filled with military personnel and trailers, was empty. There was still a barricade marked 'Evacuation Zone', but we were able to pull off near the entrance to the campground. We parked the vehicles and were quickly approached by firefighters and wildlife officers manning the line.

Alex rolled his window down. A wildlife ranger stepped up.

"This area is still under evacuation notice," he said. "Even though the fire is close to being contained, the winds have shifted back towards town. We can't be certain this area is safe yet. You're going to have to leave."

He glanced past us at the line of vehicles behind us, clearly confused.

"I completely understand your concern," I said, leaning over Alex to talk. "But we have reason to believe this property or one adjacent to it is about to have something sinister happen. We're here to check on our friend Ryan Newman. We don't believe he ever evacuated. He could be in danger."

The ranger looked at me, then at Alex, then back to me again.

"I'm sorry, miss. I can't let you in here. It's just unsafe.

"I understand. I really do. But I need to speak to whoever's in charge. Someone needs to check the house. I received a warning today that makes me believe someone could be murdered."

"Have you told the police?" he asked, eyeing me suspiciously.

"I have. Detective Parker will probably be here any minute. But in the meantime, I've brought some friends, and we really need access to this property." I answered.

"Wait here," he said, sounding annoyed.

He stepped away far enough that I could hear his radio buzz to life, but not what was being said. I assumed he was asking Incident Command how to deal with us.

Unfortunately for him, the Old Man Battalion had already begun pouring out of their vehicles. I wasn't entirely sure what their plan was.

My grandpa walked up to my door.

"Alright, lass," he said. "This is where you think the next threat is happening? Then we need to secure the area."

He started using silent hand signals, and his "troops" began fanning out.

"Grandpa, it really is still unsafe," I protested. "You can't all go running through the forest."

"Unsafe?" he scoffed. "You don't know what we've seen. This is nothing."

I scrambled out of the truck to follow them, suddenly thinking this had been a very bad idea. Robert, Alex, and Kandice were on my heels.

Moments later, an explosion ripped through the small KOA office.

Everyone ducked as bits of roofing and rocks rained down around us.

"We're under attack!" someone yelled.

Sirens wailed in the distance as fire crews were redirected towards the burning office. I stood frozen, watching the structure go up in flames, wondering if anyone was inside. Terrified that someone was.

Once the debris stopped falling and the ringing in my ears eased, the confusion only grew. The Old Man Battalion had scattered, patrolling the entire campground. Firefighters rushed to the blaze. The wildlife officer stood stunned, no doubt wondering if I had somehow caused this.

Alex's phone buzzed.

"It's David," he said, glancing at the screen.

"He's going to kill me," I sighed.

"But once again, you have an alibi. You were with me. You couldn't possibly have blown anything up." Alex smiled and took the call.

Robert leaned towards me. "I can vouch for that."

I rolled my eyes and sighed. "This is nuts."

Flames engulfed the office. I heard someone say they thought a person was inside. My heart sank. Maybe we were too late.

The fire crews charged in without hesitation. I watched in horror. After what felt like forever, they emerged carrying an unconscious man.

I crept closer, trying to see. I recognized the figure.

"Ryan!" I yelled. "Ryan!"

They loaded him onto a stretcher and moved him towards the ambulance. One of the medics rushed over, and I realized it was my brother, Scotty. I wanted to shout to him, but thought better of it.

I pushed closer until I could confirm it really was Ryan. He looked completely unresponsive.

I stood watching, praying. He coughed.

I broke through the barrier and ran to him, leaving Kandice and the boys behind.

"Ryan, what happened?" I said.

A firefighter tried to stop me, but Scotty held him back. "She's fine. Let her through."

Ryan coughed again. "Sell or burn," he rasped.

Then he slipped back into unconsciousness. Fear washed over me. I was too late. Behind me, I heard shouting.

"We've got one of them! We've got one of them!"

I ran towards the commotion.

The Old Man Battalion had surrounded a woman. She was covered in dirt and soot.

"You have to let me leave!" she demanded. "I didn't do anything. You have no authority over me."

"This is a citizen's arrest, lassie," my grandpa said. "You'll be held until Detective Parker arrives."

Recognizing that the woman was Rosie, I approached her. "Rosie, what are you doing out here?" I asked.

"Nothing," she said quickly. "Ryan asked me to come. He wanted me to take some paperwork to the police station."

That didn't make sense. Ryan had been contacting me the whole time. If he needed something taken to the police, why wouldn't he have just said so? I studied her face, trying to decide if she looked scared or just annoyed at being caught. The fire snapped and roared, sending sparks twisting into the night. Grandpa's battalion shifted positions like they were preparing for an invasion instead of a campground emergency.

Before I could press her further, sirens cut through the roar of the fire and all of the commotion as Detective Parker's cruiser skidded to a stop, lights flashing blue and red across the smoke. He didn't even seem to notice us. He was already moving towards the cluster of EMS and firefighters coordinating near the engine.

I hurried straight into his path.

"There's been a citizen's arrest?" he asked before I could speak, his eyes scanning past me towards the burning KOA office. "A female?"

"Yes," I said quickly. "The Old Man Battalion has her over there." I pointed towards groups of seventy-year-olds in fatigues and waving flashlights.

David blinked, staring past me. "The what?"

Before I could answer the question, movement behind him caught my eye. Gravel crunched behind us. A woman in heels was picking her way across the gravel.

"Who is she?" I asked, narrowing my eyes.

Parker followed my gaze. "Oh, that's Heather." He shrugged slightly. "She reminds me a lot of you."

"I take offense to that." I narrowed my eyes. "What is she doing here?"

"I can only imagine the same reason you are. She's helping. Or at least she's presented some information that would confirm Ryan as a person of interest in all of this."

I folded my arms. "Do you trust her?"

"Taryn, now's not a good time." He rubbed the back of his neck. "I had to detain Jason. He's in a holding cell waiting for questioning. His description matches the guy who bought the flowers. That, coupled with the cow-poop prank and your grandmother's rosebushes... I just need to sort all this out."

His gaze drifted past me towards the military-style operation unfolding in the dirt lot. My grandpa's makeshift battalion had formed a perimeter like they were defending a small country.

"And what," David said slowly, gesturing to the old men, "is all of this?"

"My grandpa wanted to help since my family was threatened. Some of his friends came as backup." I pushed dirt around with my toe, staring at the ground.

Detective Parker rubbed his temples. "You really do have a way of getting into trouble, don't you?"

"Hey!" I started to complain, then thought better of it and shut my mouth.

Heather was approaching quickly. She looked like she'd stepped into a courtroom instead of into a wildfire disaster, her bronze hair twisted into a very tight French twist and her dress suit crisp despite the smoke hanging in the air. She extended her hand.

"Hi, I'm Heather Katz, and you must be Taryn."

I shook her hand and smiled politely. "Why yes, I am. I'm a friend of Ryan's. How do you know him?"

"Oh, we've talked a few times. One of my clients was working with him." She smiled slightly.

"Funny," I said lightly. "I heard you have evidence against him. That he might be the criminal mastermind in all of this."

"Oh, I'm not here to point fingers." Her smile widened. "I produce evidence. It's up to the detective." She pawed at his arm, "And eventually the judge to decide what's really going on." She batted her eyes.

"Of course," I said. "Excuse me for a moment, I need to throw up."

David glared daggers at me.

I turned and scanned the chaos until I spotted Kandice near the edge of the forest. She looked like she was having a serious conversation with a pine tree. Excusing myself, I went to grab Kandice.

"What are you doing?" I whispered as I reached her.

"Trey's here," she answered.

A head popped out from behind the bushes. Trey waved enthusiastically.

"Hi, Taryn." He grinned.

I smiled. "Trey. Are you back in town now?" I gave him a wink.

"Mostly." He chuckled.

"I'll leave you alone. I need to find someone I can complain to at the moment."

"Wait," Kandice curled her hand around my arm, "What's going on?"

"Heather Katz, the attorney, just showed up. She's collecting evidence to prove Ryan is the prime suspect in all of this."

"Hold on a minute," Kandice said. "Trey, I'll see you tonight." She smiled.

"I think I'll be back in town by then." He smirked.

She grabbed him and kissed him before releasing him and following me back towards the firelight.

"So you two are all good then?" I asked.

"Yes, you were right. I was being a crazy person, and now that I have processed it all, I have decided he is so worth all of it. Plus, it was kind of cute that he found me from the bushes, too." She smiled.

"You guys are goofy, but I am so glad everything is good between you two." I smiled. "Now we need to keep an eye on Heather," I whispered. "I don't know what she's up to, and I'm not sure what's happening here."

"Agreed," Kandice replied.

We milled around, pretending to listen to conversations and trying to grab any piece of information we could while Detective Parker spoke with EMS and firefighters. Heather lingered nearby, doing the same, quietly lurking.

"Hey, Robert," I said, grabbing his sleeve. "Can you go distract Heather?"

"Who?" he looked around.

"Heather Katz. She's over there, close to David, listening to what EMS and the firefighters are saying. She claims she's building a case for him against Ryan. I'd like to know why she's so invested."

He sighed dramatically. "You know you owe me. You've got me talking to all kinds of women these days."

"You like it." I smiled. "But thank you. I do owe you."

He trudged off towards Heather.

I grabbed Alex next. I was going to use him to my advantage, too.

"Alex, Rosie seems to have a crush on you. She claims she has nothing to do with all of this, and the Old Man Battalion has her basically held hostage until David's ready to talk to her. Think you could work some magic? See what she's really up to?"

He looked at me, then at Kandice, then back at me again.

"I'll see what I can find out. But you two had better stay in this lit area. No sneaking off into the forest and doing your own thing," he warned. "I see you've occupied Robert. Now you're doing the same to me." He eyed me suspiciously.

"I promise we're not going off on our own," I said. "I just don't trust Heather. And right now, I'm not sure I trust Rosie. Not saying Ryan's innocent, but it's all starting to look very convenient. If he is guilty, fine. But we need to figure this out before somebody else has other plans."

Kandice and I headed towards my grandpa.

"Grandpa, Heather, that woman over there." I pointed towards the fire unit. "She's the attorney who came to your house the day Gramma's roses were burned. Now Jason's being detained on suspicion of doing it. What are your thoughts?"

He didn't answer right away. He stared into the wind, smoke whipping around him.

"A storm doesn't change direction without a reason," he said quietly. "They're changing for our killer." He glanced down at me. "Trust your gut, lassie. Pay close attention and see what she's up to."

Chapter 22

I looked back towards the burning KOA office, where Heather stood talking quietly with Robert, perfectly composed while everything around her burned.

A few moments later, Detective Parker approached us.

"Looks like Ryan will probably be okay," he said. "He's being transported to the hospital now. Let's talk to Rosie next. Why is she under citizen's arrest?"

David looked exhausted. The expression on his face said he could use a cup of coffee or a full night's sleep. Neither seemed to be in his immediate future. This case was clearly running him ragged.

My grandpa piped up before I could answer. "We saw her running from the scene of the crime. We got here moments before the office exploded. She was off in the forest on the trail, and she was high-tailing it out of here. My men and I stopped her. See?"

David smiled and nodded. "Thank you. Let me talk to her."

We all stood around watching. I could feel the temperature in my personal space change as Heather approached, stopping right beside me.

"This is quite the group you've got here, Taryn," she said with a smile. "Now I know if I'm ever in danger, I'll call you for help." She smirked. "It was nice meeting you, but unfortunately I've got to get going now."

Her heels clicked across the gravel as she disappeared down the driveway. Once again she looked perfectly composed as she slipped into her car and drove off.

Robert came sauntering back over. "Well? What did you find out from her?" I asked.

"Nothing damning, if that's what you were hoping for," he said. "She knows her land law. Insurance law, too. She seems convinced Ryan's the one who killed Reed. She's giving a presentation at the fairgrounds in the morning, 'Knowing Your Land Rights During a Disaster.' Apparently, she's sat in on a few council meetings lately. I'm not sure how I didn't notice her before. I mean, look at her, she's cute."

I narrowed my eyes at him. "Yeah. In a she-devil kind of way," I snipped.

He chuckled. "The only thing that felt slightly off was that she seemed very concerned about Ryan's health. When EMS said they thought he'd probably pull through, I don't know. I got the feeling she wasn't happy about that. Now, that could just be something you've put in my head because you don't like her, because otherwise, she was delightful."

I narrowed my eyes even more. "Something doesn't feel right about her. Just because she's pretty and put together doesn't mean she's not a problem. Could it be that you're the one being hoodwinked?" I asked.

Robert raised his hands. "I don't know. I doubt it. But I can't say it hasn't happened before." He grinned.

I rolled my eyes and turned my attention back to David, Rosie, and Alex. Kandice was still standing at my side.

Rosie couldn't explain why she was out there beyond saying Ryan had asked her to get papers and bring them to Detective Parker.

"And where are these papers you're supposed to give me?" David asked.

Rosie had nothing in her hands. "I got here and smelled smoke," she said. "I got scared. Moments later, the building blew up, so I took off running. I never actually got the papers, Detective."

"Smelled smoke, how could you not? We are right next to a forest fire," I grumbled to myself.

Kandice shushed me. "I am trying to listen."

"I'm sure you didn't," David muttered. "This just keeps getting crazier. There's a whole lot going on right now. I need you to come down to the station, answer a few questions, and make a statement."

She sniffed and nodded.

A couple of the old men escorted her and David to his car. Soon they were pulling away, headed towards the station, leaving the rest of us standing in the smoky aftermath while firefighters worked to finish putting out the blaze.

"All right, lassie. What's your next plan of action?" Grandpa asked as he approached me.

The problem was, I didn't have one.

"I don't know just yet." We all stood there in awkward silence while I thought as hard as I could, trying to figure out what our next move should be. Then I realized I still had one more job for the Old Man Battalion.

"Grandpa, I do have an idea."

It took me a minute to say it out loud. "Robert talked to Heather. One thing that felt slightly off was that she may have been concerned Ryan would live. I know that's not much to go on, but could a couple of your guys go down to the hospital and make sure he's secure and safe? Just in case this was an attempt on his life? And secondly, you need to get home. I'm not sure if your house will be attacked again or not. This whole evening is becoming very unsettling," I said.

Grandpa put his arm around me. "Anytime you need military backup, Lassie, you know you can count on us."

"All right, men, fall in!" he barked. "This battalion is now on hold and on notice. We could be needed again. I need two volunteers to go to the hospital and protect Ryan. He's one of ours. Since we don't really know what's going on yet, we need to do some recon and regroup. Who can go tonight?"

A couple of men stepped forward.

"Excellent. If you need a shift change, you just call. Fall out."

The old men shuffled back to their military vehicles, the rolling museum slowly exiting the KOA grounds, leaving Alex, Robert, Kandice, and me standing there, a little stunned.

"That was eventful," Alex commented.

"It was. Did Rosie tell you anything?" I asked.

"No. She said she received a text from Ryan asking her to retrieve a file folder from the office labeled 'For Detective Parker.' But she never made it inside. The office exploded before she could."

"Well, if that's true, thank God she wasn't in there," I said, blowing out a sigh.

I glanced back once more at the smoldering ruins.

"You heard Grandpa," I said. "Let's roll out."

Looking back towards the burning structure, my heart sank. Is this what Ryan meant by 'substantial damage'? The fire crew had put out most of the flames. They were on the offensive with the fire now. My brother, Scotty, left with the Fire EMS ambulance. We climbed back into the truck, and Alex drove us home. The drive back to town was quiet. Each of us was lost in our own thoughts. I felt the puzzle coming together in my brain, but some of the pieces didn't set right. Before I knew it, we were home, and the adrenaline rush we had was turning to exhaustion.

I opened my door and stepped out into the smoke-filled night. The orange glow wasn't as ominous as it once was. The fire was losing the battle. Kandice hopped out of the truck, shutting her door.

"I am going to head home, take care of Fluffy, and hopefully Trey will show up." She bounced a little on her heels.

I was happy to see that all was right in her world again. Trey had a way of calming her eccentric qualities. They were good together.

"Okay," I leaned in and hugged her. "I will call you if anything happens. I doubt anything will. David has a station full of suspects to deal with." I smiled.

"That's what I figured, so I feel it's safe to say our investigation will pick up tomorrow." She winked. "Alex, Robert, see you tomorrow." She climbed into her Jeep and drove away, waving.

Giselle was dancing back and forth in the entryway when we got in. "Hello, sweet girl," I said, entering.

"She's not that sweet," Robert complained. "Last night, she bit me because I didn't get up and refill her food the moment she asked. Look. See?" He pointed to the tiniest red dot on his hand.

"She didn't break the skin. That was a love bite," I said, picking her up, kissing her, and setting her on the couch.

"Once you two are tucked in, I am heading to the station to help David," Alex announced, heading to the kitchen.

It didn't surprise me, since he and David often worked together. I was actually happy because he might come home with answers.

"Okay." I followed him. "If I come up with something David should know, I'll text you."

Grabbing me, he pulled me in for a long kiss. "Please don't go anywhere without me," he said, his honey eyes peering into me and melting me.

"I won't, I promise," I whispered, our noses touching, and I meant it too.

Robert cleared his throat, ruining our moment.

"Yes?" Alex pulled away.

I rolled my eyes, shook my head, and smiled. Having Robert as a roommate is both annoying and fun at the same time. I am not sure why, but it sort of worked.

"Oh, nothing. I just needed to clear my throat." He smiled.

I narrowed my eyes. My phone started buzzing. I was my mom. I was so dead for letting my grandpa and his buddies go to the KOA.

"Hi mom. I can explain," I said before she could even say hello. "I needed to go out to the KOA, and Grandpa's friends wanted something to do." I tried really hard to downplay events tonight, but she wasn't buying it. My grandpa had ratted me out.

"Your grandpa said you need backup because something sinister was going down at the KOA. Then I found out there was an explosion. Your grandpa formed a militia, and now they are at the hospital!" She ranted, rightfully so.

"Look, Mom, they weren't going to listen to me," I said, thinking, here you go, Grandpa, the bus is coming for you now.

"I figured that since I was already going out to the KOA to warn Ryan that they could come." I defended my actions like I was a teenager again.

"Taryn, I am running out of things to clean," she sighed. "You and your brother are always in danger. This is not a mother's dream."

"Mom. I know all of this sounds crazy, but I promise everything will be okay. Grandpa and his friends were really helpful. Plus, I think they had more fun than they've had in a long time." I tried to sound convincing.

"Taryn, your grandpa has plenty of fun at the VFW," she protested.

"Mom, I understand, but it's late. Let's talk about this tomorrow, please," I pleaded.

"Fine, but I don't expect to get much sleep."

"I love you," I said.

"Love you too, honey." My mother sighed before hanging up.

"That didn't sound good." Robert smirked.

"Nope, I knew my mother was going to kill me, but I didn't think my grandpa would rat me out." I blew out a sigh.

"I am seeing a common thread here," Alex grinned.

"Don't," I said. "Keep your opinions to your-self."

"Okay, I am heading out then." Alex's smile grew wider before he leaned in and kissed me goodbye.

I watched from my office window as he drove away, Robert leaning in the doorway. "What is your plan?" he asked.

"I am going to make a list of what we know and try to find the connection." I grabbed my notepad off my desk. "I know it's there, staring me in the face," I said, brushing past him.

He grabbed my hand. "Do you ever wish things would go back the way they were?" he asked.

Pulling my hand away, I looked at him. "Do you mean us?" I asked.

"Us, no investigations, no party planning, a world where you were never kidnapped," he answered.

"Sometimes, yes," I said hesitantly. "But for whatever reason, this is the path we have been placed on, and the only choice we have is to move forward. Looking back won't help." I offered him a smile as I moved past him.

"I guess you are right." He pushed off the doorway and followed me to the dining room table.

"Robert, we all make choices based on our emotions at that moment. Sometimes they are good and sometimes not so much." I patted the chair next to me. "Let's see if we can figure out which one of these people has made bad choices." I scribbled the names of everyone involved, making columns. Inside each column, I wrote what we knew to be true about each. From there, I put their suspicious activity, and then the facts we had went into the next row.

I had a grid of notes. Looking at my bouquet, I started moving those pieces together.

Robert looked up the company Obsidian, and after a deep dive into the internet, it looked like they were an investment firm and partnered with Camp World, Little Helper Farms, and Neighborhood Integrity, among many more companies. They helped with partnerships of smaller companies that want to work with their larger corporate partners. That would make sense why Jason would have been listed as a partner on his permit, and it could be why the military was poking around these fires. They would want to know what their investments were up to. I made a column for Obsidian, putting a mark next to Jason's name. The paper trail was leading to Heather's firm, but the fires and Reed's death still looked like it really could be Ryan, with tonight's fire being the exception.

But how did my gramma's rose bushes fit into all of this? And what about the Thompsons? Were they really only in this because of the rezoning push?

We went round and round, discussing our scenarios until the early hours of the morning before finally calling it off. I would regroup with Alex in the morning. He will know what Rosie and Jason said. Once Ryan was cleared, he would have to make a statement as well.

With Robert tucked into my couch, and my mean cat curled up on top of him, I went to bed.

Chapter 23

Heather had a presentation scheduled for 10 a.m. this morning at the fairgrounds. The news had just announced that the KOA fire was seventy percent contained, and they were hoping to let residents return by tomorrow morning. The fairgrounds exhibit hall, that had been home to a fair amount of Silver Springs residents over the last few days, was buzzing, partly with excitement of the thought of being able to return home, partly with the fear of what had really been going on in our town. Rumors about Ryan killing Reed, setting the fires, and even burning his own property, spread through the crowd like wildfire. Jason's involvement in the liquor license mess was being whispered about, too. Each story growing wilder than the last.

Cots, backpacks, duffel bags, and crated pets filled the room. In the back corner, close to the kitchen, a little lunch area had been set up. Alex and I served food here only a few days earlier. A makeshift stage was set up just beyond the lunch area. A podium and three rows of chairs hugged the wall. The overspill of listeners would sit at the lunch tables. Alex, Robert, and I were already seated when Kandice and Trey showed up. He had arrived home this morning. His 'mission' was over. Detective Parker stood in the corner, quietly observing the crowd. I waved, and he gave me a short nod. I had called the Old Man Battalion in on one more job. They had the fairgrounds surrounded.

Amy slid in next to me and whispered, "They found Reed's killer. It was Ryan Newman. I can't believe it. I've known him for years," she said, her voice low. "And I know they fought. Heather told me he was under a lot of financial stress, and with the insurance rates rising, the KOA needed to be sold. He finally just snapped, couldn't take it any longer. He took his anger out on Reed." She started to tear up. "Hopefully those nasty rumors will die down now, but some people still think Reed did all of this."

I patted her shoulder. "Don't worry. The truth will come out. People will understand."

She smiled faintly. "I hope you're right."

"With Reed gone, are you still going to work for Suds and Scrubs?" I asked.

"Well, I hadn't really thought about it. Sheila is so sweet, I wouldn't want to up and leave her, but I never wanted to work for her either. I guess I'd better have a conversation with my husband," she said.

"There's time for everything, don't worry about it right now," I said, patting her hand.

"I guess you're right."

We chatted quietly until Councilman Thompson appeared at the podium. "Citizens of Silver Springs," he began, "these last few days have been challenging, but our community stuck together, like we always do. We're resilient. We're a community of love and passion. Hopefully, we will be receiving the good news that the fire is contained and you can return home soon. Today, I'd like to introduce Heather Katz and her colleague, Marco Salgner. They've been assisting with land value assessments, insurance mediation, and advising the council on rebuilding and planning for the future of Silver Springs. Today, they're here to speak about 'Knowing Your Land Rights During A Disaster'. Hopefully, this presentation will answer some of the questions you may have and explain how to navigate what's ahead for our small town." He smiled. "So, with the support of this beautiful community, let's give them a warm welcome."

Applause filled the room as Heather stepped up to the podium, impeccably composed. She talked about disaster rebuilding limitations, inspections, and sometimes forced transactions. My eyes wandered, trying not to drift off while waiting for the Q&A session. Then she referenced the KOA office: "Once the KOA office was destroyed, grandfathered-in codes and inspection rights could be removed because the surrounding land had to comply. To rebuild, you must be compliant as well."

Members of the crowd shook their heads in disbelief. People began asking questions, and I raised my hand. Heather nodded. This was it. If I was going to get her to slip up, it would be because she believed she was still the smartest person in the room.

"Would you normally prepare zoning arguments before an official damage assessment is complete?" I asked.

She smiled, completely unfazed. "Preparation is part of responsible legal practice. Disasters create uncertainty, and clients often want to understand potential outcomes before formal reports are issued. It doesn't mean a decision has been made, just simply to ensure that they aren't caught unprepared."

Perfect, I thought, she's taking the bait. She was building the very foundation I needed her to. "And if an inspection officer were removed from the situation?" I asked. "Is there any disruption that could slow administrative timelines?"

She answered, tilting her head slightly, as if she was enjoying the question. "Inspections must be documented, reviewed, and sometimes reassigned. Procedures exist to prevent a single individual from holding up a determination. The system is designed to move forward."

I nodded and pressed on. She had to slip up sometime. "And if someone attended council meetings and drafted legal language before a disaster occurred, what would that suggest?"

A few people murmured around me.

She stiffened slightly, adjusting the microphone at the podium. "It would suggest foresight," she said confidently. "Land use policy doesn't appear overnight. Attorneys, developers, and municipalities often monitor long-term trends, preparing ahead to help communities respond quickly when change is inevitable." She shifted her weight and straightened her suit coat.

"And if an attorney also had clients who would benefit from the land becoming available?" I asked a little more cautiously. I could see her getting more uncomfortable with each question I asked.

Her smile tightened. "That would be disclosed according to professional ethics. Representing multiple interests in redevelopment scenarios isn't unusual. My role is to provide lawful options, not determine the path a property ultimately takes."

"So why were you preparing land transition arguments before the fire even happened?" I jabbed a bit harder.

Heather moved her hair back. "I wasn't preparing arguments about this fire," she said. "I was advising clients about regional expansion possibilities. We all know we're in a wildfire zone. When communities grow, difficult transitions occur. Unfortunately, sometimes events accelerate them."

"The expansion packet and land assessment were filed with the city the day the fire started, and your office blocked the search for Reed's body." I argued. The tension in the room was becoming palpable. Residents began whispering among themselves.

Her composure faltered, the first crease of defensiveness showing. "That was standard protocol," she said, clasping her hands tightly. "Client privilege sometimes requires careful handling of sensitive information, especially in cases involving potential liability. It was never intended to obstruct anyone, merely to protect privacy while the authorities conducted their work."

The audience shifted in their seats. The whispers grew louder. Heather's calm exterior was starting to crack.

Before I could ask another question, Jason stood up from the crowd. "Ms. Katz," he said, "help me understand something. I was being harassed, my liquor license threatened. I had to get a permit for Camp World, a future property, just to keep everything legit. Did someone from your office get involved with this, too?"

Heather forced a smile. "Yes. We provide guidance to ensure all legal requirements are met. My role is to make sure clients understand their options and comply with regulations, especially when licenses or permits might be challenged."

She began fidgeting with the edge of the podium. That was when Rosie stepped forward.

"Ms. Katz," Rosie said, "I have another question about something I found while helping my friend, and I actually bought it with me." Rosie held up the wax-sealed envelope that she had taken from the KOA office at Ryan's request. It's a note from your office along with a copy of the state-issued permit for Mr. Moon's liquor license at Camp World. Can you explain why your office would be handling this before any disaster happened, and why it ended up being delivered to Ryan Newman's office yesterday?"

Heather stepped back from the podium, her eyes cut to Marco Salgner, her partner, and then to Councilman Thompson. Before she could explain, Detective Parker stepped forward.

"Heather Katz, you're under arrest for the murder of Reed Jackson, the attempted murder of Ryan Newman, arson of Mrs. McCarthy's rose bushes, an attempt to frame Mr. Moon and possibly of leaving a flaming bag of poop on Miss O'Kelly's doorstep." he announced, cracking a slight smile. "Marco Salgner, you're being brought in for questioning, as you were confirmed to have delivered a death threat to Miss O'Kelly."

Heather tried to bolt. She flung open the emergency exit doors on the side of the stage and was met by two old men in uniform, one wielding a cane. There was no escape. The Old Man Battalion had surrounded the building. She froze like a deer in headlights. There was nothing she could do.

"Your town should thank me!" she raged, whirling around to face the crowd. "I stopped Reed! He set those fires. He was out of control. Someone had to stop him. Your entire town would've burned down if it weren't for me," she snarled. "Everything was going along just perfectly. He and I were an excellent team, denying your petty claims and ushering in reasonable partners like Camp World and Little Help Farms. Your zoning, and land development is about to go through. We were about to put Silver Springs on the map! Without us, you'll be nothing."

Detective Parker handcuffed her and read her her rights. He and Officer Ballenger escorted both Heather and Marco to their car. The battalion flanked the edges to prevent escape. Councilman Thompson looked shocked. I wasn't sure how much he really knew about what was going on, or how much Heather had manipulated him, too, but just to be safe, Grandpa and one of his military buddies remained close by. He would need to be brought in for questioning as well.

Amy turned to me. "How did you figure it all out? How did you know it was Heather all along?" she asked.

"I didn't at first. She did a very good job manipulating a lot of people, as did Reed. They probably would've gotten away with it, too, had Reed not gone off the rails and set too many fires. I knew in my gut Ryan couldn't be the one who did it. He may be a little different, a lone wolf of sorts. But I knew he loved this town too much to have done something like this." I smiled, "However, when you confessed to me that you didn't even want the job at Sud and Scrubs, and that you were looking for financial documents, I knew Heather had to have been involved somehow. She was trying to cover her tracks, seeing if Reed had left any evidence of their collusion."

"And what's going to happen to my husband?" Amy asked.

"Well, now we'll find out how much he really knew. But unfortunately, I think his career as a councilman in this town is probably over. I can't see how many people will trust him again. For that, I am sorry," I apologized.

She hugged me. "I know it seems weird to say, with my husband possibly facing charges, but thank you. This whole thing had me feeling so uneasy and so stressed that I was sick. To be through it all now, and to have closure, I know we can move on, and we'll be fine. One thing I will say about my husband: he may have been manipulated, but he does love Silver Springs. That, I can be sure of."

The exhibit hall had gone silent during the arrest, residents unsure how to react, not sure what to say with the unsettling news, but as soon as Heather was removed, the chatter filled the room again.

Alex leaned over and patted my shoulder, "Good job, Sherlock. I don't know how your mind works, but it works differently than the rest of ours."

Kandice smirked. "That's because she's an angel," she said.

Robert joined us. "Hey, I didn't think you were Charlie's Angels anymore. Detective Parker dubbed us Mystery Inc. Plus, it took all of us, did it not?" He laughed.

Rosie was lurking nearby. I left my group and approached her. "Hey, when I asked why you weren't here the other day, were you really just out?" I asked.

"I was," she answered with a shrug. "Running errands, getting snacks. I mean, it's no fun hanging out here all day."

"Margery said you never checked in." I eyed her. "Why would she tell me that?" I asked. This was the only piece to the puzzle I hadn't wrapped my head around.

Rosie smiled. "My real name's Rosalina Sanchez-Sullivan. That's what I was checked in under."

I eyed her. She was an odd one, but if it weren't for the wax-sealed note, I may not have fully connected the dots. "Well, thank you. I know Ryan owes his life to you."

She giggled, "I am just glad it's all over. I'll see you around, Taryn." She skipped off towards Alex.

I watched her go, spotting Jason heading for the exit. I hadn't talked to him since before he was detained.

"Hey Jason, wait!" I called out.

He stopped, turning around.

"Why didn't you tell us about your liquor license?" I asked him quietly as I approached him. "You played like you didn't know what was going on."

Jason shrugged. "I knew if it got out that I had already retained a permit for a future Camp World, suspicion would turn towards me if something happened to the KOA. It would look like I had something to gain." He glanced towards the fairground's doors. "I didn't know for sure Heather was involved as deeply as she was, but I knew something wasn't right. Not with her. Not with Thompson. Not with Reed. They were all suspicious. I was protecting myself. But I also knew you'd have to figure this out eventually, so I gave you just enough information."

"It would've been easier," I muttered, "if you had just given me your license information before the KOA blew up."

Jason gave a helpless half-smile. "It wouldn't have mattered. She still used it against me. For the record, I have never put flaming poop on someone's doorstep. Showing my butt is one thing, but poop, that's a bridge too far."

"Well, if it makes you feel any better, my mother knew you were innocent the whole time." I smiled.

"You didn't?" he questioned.

"I never believed it was you, but Heather did work a lot of things out perfectly. She knew you would be walking past my parents' house once the speakeasy closed. She definitely paid attention." I shuddered. "Your permit played into her hands to make Ryan look guilty. The raging lone wolf camp owner goes crazy and kills local adjuster."

"Why do you think she framed me for that?" he asked. The crowd was beginning to thin.

"We made her mad. You, me, Alex, my gramma, everyone, really. She thought she had everything under control. She cracked. You were right about people watching." I smiled.

"I see a lot of things. People don't always take me as seriously as they should." He smiled. "One of the advantages of being the town mooner."

"Next time, don't be so cryptic. You're pretty good at this!" I chuckled.

Jason grinned and turned around to leave. He pulled just a tiny corner of his pants down at me before pulling it back up, chuckling, and making his exit.

I shook my head. What a dork, I thought. I went to round up Grandpa and the Old Man Battalion. They were finally being released from their self-appointed security duties, and honestly, they were so helpful. I will have to remember this the next time I face off with a killer, because whether I want to or not, I am sure there will be another one.

"Hi, Grandpa," I said, wrapping my arms around him.

"Thanks, Lassie. You made us feel important again." He placed his arm around me. "I know your mom and gramma were worried," Grandpa admitted. "Most of the guys' wives were. But we had it under control." He grinned. "This was one of the best times we've had in years." His soft hand brushed my cheek. "I love you, Lassie."

"I love you too, Grandpa." I hugged him tight. "Mom and Gramma will be okay with everything, especially now that the killer has been taken into custody. I'll swing by later and talk to them."

"They will like that." He nodded and shuffled off to his buddies. No doubt, they were headed to the VFW to retell their latest adventure story.

I shook my head, smiling.

"I guess you were right to include them," Alex said, sneaking quietly up beside me.

"It was probably a little too dangerous," I admitted. "But they seemed to be happy. Sometimes people just need to feel useful again."

"They will always be needed. They just might not realize it." He smiled.

"Is Rosie good?" I asked.

"She's fine. Thanks for ditching me." He nudged my shoulder playfully.

"No, problem." I smiled. "I still can't believe she went out to the office to get the file Ryan was putting together. It's a good thing she checked the outside drop box before she entered. It saved her life."

"I don't think Heather planned on that. Rosie was a wildcard she hadn't accounted for. When Ryan was onto Heather, she knew she had to get rid of him like she did Reed. Rosie was just in the right place at the wrong time."

Across the hall, I spotted Robert speaking with Councilman Thompson.

"Come on," Alex said. "Let's see what he plans to do next."

Oliver Thompson stiffened when we approached.

"Mr. Thomson, this is Alex, my boyfriend," I said, introducing them.

"So this is the fancy new PI in town helping you to do your snooping in things you don't belong in," he muttered.

Alex's jaw tightened.

"I don't snoop for fun," I said calmly. "I am perfectly happy planning parties until people like you try to ruin them. I get involved when people leave me no choice." I could feel a little Irish rage brewing inside me.

"She is very smart. She doesn't need me to figure out when a scam is happening." Alex replied sharply.

Oliver Thompson narrowed his eyes at us, trying not to react.

"I assume you'll be resigning," I said, breaking the silence.

"I'm preparing my resignation letter this afternoon," he replied. "And for the record, Miss Nosy, I had nothing to do with Reed's or Heather's activities. Silver Springs needs to grow. Camp World and Little Helper Farms are coming whether you like it or not." He turned away. "I have a public announcement to make."

Robert watched him go, a grin spreading slowly across his face. "There's going to be a seat on the city council opening up soon." He tucked his hands into his pockets.

"You're not thinking of running for council, are you?" I asked.

"Why not?" He shrugged. "I go to most meetings, anyway. I like wining and dining people. And I want to protect our town. Maybe I should?"

I looked at him, thinking for a moment, "Honestly, you'd probably do an excellent job." I said, grabbing his hand, come on, let's go home.

I walked out of the exhibit hall holding each of my boys' hands. Our little team did well.

Outside, I noticed reporter Racheal Post interviewing Kandice and Trey. She motioned for us to come over.

"How do you do it?" she asked.

I glanced at Alex, at Robert, and at Kandice and Trey. "I have a great team, but I think I know someone with a better story you may want to interview," I said.

She looked at me, confused, "Who?"

"My grandpa and the boys at the VFW. They'll have fun details to tell you."

"But aren't you going to make a statement?" she questioned.

I smiled. "If anyone threatens my town or my family, we will find you, and we will make sure justice is served. Remember that before you try anything cruel. Party planning is my name. Body finding is the game."

The boys burst out laughing as we walked away, leaving Racheal taking notes on her notepad.

Chapter 24

I had promised Grandpa I would go see Mom. Kandice and Trey had 'things to discuss', AKA they were behaving like rabbits now that everything was patched up between them. Robert went to inquire about honorary councilmanship. That left Alex and me. We pulled up to my parents' house. My gramma's burned bushes looked so sad, but before we even got to the door, my gramma popped out. "You have to come see this!" She grabbed my hands and ushered me down the steps around the side of the house to the garden. "Look, she didn't kill them." She pointed to the little green saplings pushing through the charred branches. "Somehow they survived, but the most beautiful part is this." She pointed to my great-great-grandmother's memory stone. A single pink bud was opening just above it.

"Oh, Gramma," I gasped, "thank heavens," I said, giving her a tight hug.

"Faith," Gramma said softly.

A tear slid down my cheek. Wiping it away, I looked up and whispered, "Thank you," to God.

My gramma squeezed my hand. "Now come on inside. Your mother has taken to baking. She didn't have anything left to clean when you freaked her out again. So she decided she had to start baking. She's made pecan rolls, cinnamon rolls, and blueberry muffins. She is even trying her hand at croissants. Your father couldn't be happier. We'll see if she's put away the chemicals for good, but I fear we'll all be fat if she has," my gramma said, laughing.

I smiled softly. "I guess I'm glad some things may have changed from all the chaos I continue to find myself in."

"Did you say pecan rolls?" Alex asked my gramma.

"Sure did," she replied. "The real gooey, delicious kind."

"I've been wanting those all week," he said with a smile.

Gramma escorted us into the house. It smelled almost as good as the bakery downtown. No wonder my dad is happy. I rolled my eyes and smiled to myself. I love this family.

"Molly! Taryn and Alex are here!" my gramma shouted.

My mother came rushing out of the kitchen, nearly knocking me over as she pulled me into a tight hug. Then she turned and hugged Alex, too.

"Thank God you're safe," she said. "And taking on another killer!?"

"We make a pretty good team, Mom," I said, looking at Alex and smiling.

"That you do," she smiled. "Now come have some delicious pastries and tell me how you figured this whole thing out."

We sat at the little breakfast table, and my mom served us pastry after pastry. We told the story between bites of pastries and laughter.

"Oh, Grandpa said he was happy to be a part of it. He hadn't felt that important in a long time." I mentioned.

My mother smiled. "You spoil him. You know that."

"Well, without his help, this could've been more difficult to do," Alex piped up, as he dug into a second pecan roll. "Actually, if they hadn't grabbed Rosie when they did, who knows what would've happened. She might not have made it to David with the evidence. There were a lot of moving parts in this case, lots of things hanging on one another. The outcome could've been very different."

By the time we finished breakfast, or I should say lunch, I was exhausted, and I still needed to check in with Ryan. It had been a long four days. We thanked my gramma and my mother for the delicious pastry assortment and left. All was right in their world again. Exiting the house, I glanced over at the rose garden one more time. A smile spread across my face.

"Off to see Ryan," I said.

Alex opened the truck door for me, and I climbed in. The drive to the hospital was short enough. When we arrived at Ryan's room, one of the Old Man Battalion members stood from the little chair outside the door. "Miss Taryn," he saluted me.

I smiled. "Heather has been apprehended, you don't have to stay," I said.

"I know, miss, but I'll feel better once he is released. It should be later today," he replied, his wrinkling skin and shortening body statue standing proud.

"Thank you for your service," I hugged him, and we entered Ryan's room.

"Thank you, sir." Alex shook his hand and gave him a gentle pat on the shoulder.

Ryan was sitting up, watching a Family Feud rerun, and eating lime Jell-O. He grabbed the remote, turned the TV off, and motioned for us to sit.

"How are you feeling?" I asked, taking a seat in the nearby chair.

"Not bad for being blown up." He smiled, "Heather was clearly not the arsonist mastermind that Reed was. If she had been, I wouldn't be here."

"When did you discover it was Heather?" I asked.

"That night we all went out, and your friend was upset that her civilian military boy was involved in this. I started suspecting her involvement because she was out there, talking to the guys in the camper by my office," he said, taking a scoop of green Jell-O.

"Why didn't you say anything?" I asked.

"I warned you to stay out of it. I was worried you would end up like Reed. I started poring through all of the paperwork from the last few months. I snuck in and out of that camp the whole time, trying to piece it all together." He stopped to take another bite of Jell-O.

Alex and I leaned forward in our chairs. I eyed Ryan, "I tracked down the expansion packet the same day we met a second time, and you said you were grandfathered in."

"Exactly, you see why I couldn't leave. I wasn't one hundred percent sure it was her, but I knew the KOA would eventually be under attack. If I waited long enough, I figured if it was her, she would reveal herself."

"And what about Reed's body? It was moved." I questioned.

"Yeah, weird. I never did see what happened there, but I was in the parking lot with you when he disappeared." He shifted slightly in the hospital bed. "Detective Parker said the autopsy showed that he was most likely pushed into the ravine, and the trauma to the head is what ultimately killed him."

"Heather had to have seen me and Kandice then." I shuddered at the thought. "No wonder she was watching me."

"Taryn, sorry I was so grumpy the last time we spoke. I really didn't want you involved. After what happened to you last fall, I couldn't risk it," he apologized.

"Thank you," Alex said.

"Yeah, thanks for trying to keep me safe, even at your own risk." I smiled, standing. "We will let you get some rest."

We exited his room and waved goodbye to his guard. I looked at Alex. "This whole thing was bananas," I said.

"Interesting events, that's for sure." He smiled, grabbing my hand and escorting me out.

That evening, evacuation orders were finally lifted. Robert was free to go home.

With his bag packed and his pillow under his arm, he handed me my key. "Thanks for trusting me." He smiled.

A strange sadness settled in my chest. He had only been my roommate for a few days, but the thought of him not being here daily felt heavier than I expected. I pushed those feelings aside. "I haven't been on a run in days. Want to go for a run before you leave?" I asked.

He smirked. "I thought you'd never ask."

We ran the Riverwalk like old times, summer flowers beginning to bloom again. The town felt at peace. We ran side by side in comfortable silence, letting the fresh air clear our lungs and our minds. Once we returned home, he kissed me on the cheek, said goodbye, and drove away in the red Corvette. I smiled. He had become a good friend.

Alex was doing paperwork in my office when I walked back into the house.

"How was the run?" He poked his head out of my office.

"Great! Everything is so much better when I run. I am going to jump in the shower. I'll be out in a few minutes."

He grabbed me for a kiss as I walked by.

I could smell Alex cooking something after I got out of the shower, and I got a wicked idea. I slipped on the dress Robert had gotten me, leaving the underwear behind, of course.

"I didn't get the attention I deserved while wearing this the other night," I announced with a sly grin.

"No, you did not. In my defense, we had a house full." He smiled. "It took everything in my body not to rip it off you."

"Well, no one's here now." I smirked. "But don't rip the dress."

He grabbed me and kissed me with a lot of tongue, working his kisses down my collarbone. Sweeping me off my feet, he took me to the bedroom.

I am going to have to wear this dress more often!

One week later

The KOA reopening picnic was a huge success. I called a local bakery and asked them to cater s'mores cups since we all felt that campfires or bonfires weren't something anybody was quite ready for. But how can you have a campground party without s'mores, right? They happily obliged.

At the little pavilion, Mayor Wilson stood, gathering a large crowd of campers and picnickers together to make an announcement.

"I am so happy to be here today for the reopening of the KOA campground, a staple in the heart of Silver Springs, and to be standing here with Ryan and Taryn, who refused to give up despite continued threats. This town is about community, love, and the great outdoors. Thank you, everyone, for being here." He paused before continuing. "As for Councilman Thompson, there has been a full investigation into what he actually knew and what he didn't know. He has formally resigned from his position. In the meantime, an honorary councilman has been selected: Robert Campbell. He has agreed to take the position until the elections this fall." He motioned for Robert to come forward.

Robert sauntered up to the podium, waving at the crowd. His charismatic smile was radiating from him. He looked good in the spotlight.

"Citizens of Silver Springs, I am proud to live in this valley. I grew up here, and I love this town. I will do my best to serve you with honor. Thank you."

The crowd cheered and applauded. The mayor turned the mic over to Ryan. "Ryan has a few words."

Stepping forward, Ryan took the mic. "I know most of you never doubted me, not in your hearts. I just want to thank you for giving me another chance and allowing me to rebuild the campground the way it was. This campground has been a healing place for me and for many. Thank you."

As the crowd slowly drifted towards the s'mores table, the sound of laughter filled the campground once more. Silver Springs was healing. Ryan was rebuilding. Robert was already being stopped by half the town with congratulations. Alex stood beside me, warm and comforting as always.

Then, near the entrance of the campground, a dark SUV rolled quietly past, no logos, no license plate. Just tinted windows, but for a brief moment the sunlight caught the small silver emblem on the back. A shard of black glass set inside a circle. Obsidian. The vehicle disappeared down the valley road before I could say a word. Maybe it meant nothing. Silver Springs was growing. New investors. New visitors. New plans. Still...

Summer had finally arrived in Colorado. The season was shaping up to be a busy one, but the best part was that our town had survived wildfires, attempted corporate buyouts, and political disaster. I was proud of all of us. I sat at my desk, planning what I hoped would be a completely dead-body-free event, when the familiar tapping started again. The annoying woodpecker.

Giselle noticed it too. She had been sleeping peacefully in her hammock, but sprang to attention and dashed across my desk towards the windowsill, assuming her flat-faced attack position.

"Silly cat," I muttered, shaking my head.

When I looked back outside, I noticed something I hadn't seen before. The woodpecker wasn't alone. Two tiny fledglings clung awkwardly to the side of the tree beside her.

"Aww... she's a momma," I said softly.

I picked up Giselle and held her against my shoulder. "We can't hate on her. She's just feeding her kids."

Giselle wriggled in protest, clearly convinced I had lost my mind, and tried to escape. I set her back in her hammock, where she continued to glare at both me and the tree.

I wandered back to the window, watching the determined little bird continue her relentless work.

"Please don't kill my tree," I told her.

With a small sigh and a smile, I returned to my desk. I had a lot of party planning to do.

The End

Thank You!

Thank you so much for reading. I hope you enjoyed the story.

I'd truly appreciate an honest review. Reviews help other readers discover books they might love, and they mean more to authors than you know.

For your convenience, you can **visit SaltyInspirations.com/books/ or scan the QR code below** to leave a review.

About the author

Michelle L. Clifton was raised in southwest Colorado in the great valleys of the Rocky Mountains. There, she married the love of her life and raised two beautiful kids, along with a cat, two dogs, and a flock of chickens.

Over the years, Michelle has worked in the dental field, the dance and theater industry, athletics, and event coordinating. She created *Salty Inspirations* to pursue her passion for writing, though her favorite job will always be being Mom.

Her family made a major move to Cape Coral, Florida, just in time for Hurricane Ian. These days, they split their free time between hiking and camping in Colorado and boating and beaching in Florida.

Oh, and writing, of course!

Connect with Michelle

Visit me online at Saltyinspirations.com

Love mystery, mischief, and exclusive bookish perks? Sign up for my monthly newsletter for the latest updates on the Taryn O'Kelly Mysteries, upcoming events, sneak peeks, and freebies just for subscribers!

Follow me here:
Facebook/authorMichelleLClifton
Instagram
Michelle L Clifton @ salty_inspirations_
YouTube/saltyinspirations
Pinterest/saltyinspirations
Goodreads/MichelleLClifton

Next In The Series

A Taryn O'Kelly Mystery – Book 4

Taryn and the gang will return next spring in a brand-new Silver Springs mystery and this time, the stakes are higher than ever.

www.ingramcontent.com/pod-product-compliance
Lightning Source LLC
Chambersburg PA
CBHW020320180726
47991CB00018B/140